Tame M

A Stark International Novella

By J. Kenner

EVIL EYE
CONCEPTS

Tame Me
A Stark International Novella
By J. Kenner

Copyright 2014 Julie Kenner
ISBN: 978-1-940887-03-6

Published by Evil Eye Concepts, Incorporated

This is a work of fiction. Names, places, characters and incidents are the product of the author's imagination and are fictitious. Any resemblance to actual persons, living or dead, events or establishments is solely coincidental.

Chapter One

That, I think, *was one hell of a party.*

I am standing with my back to the Pacific as I watch the efficient crew break down the lovely white tents. The leftover food has already been packed away. The trash has been discarded. The band left hours ago, and the last of the guests have already departed.

Even the paparazzi who had camped out on the beach hoping to snag a few choice pictures of my best friend Nikki Fairchild's wedding to multi-bazillionaire and former tennis star Damien Stark are long gone.

I sigh and tell myself that this vague emptiness I'm feeling isn't melancholy. Instead, it's an aftereffect of staying up all night drinking and partying. I am, of course, lying. I'm melancholy as shit, but I figure that's normal. After all, I've just watched my best friend get married to the one man in the entire universe who is absolutely, positively perfect for her. Great news, and I'm really and truly happy for her, but she found him without trolling through the entire male population of Los Angeles.

Compare that to me, who's fucked approximately eighty percent of that population and still hasn't found a guy like Damien, and I think it's safe to say that Nikki got the last decent man.

Okay, maybe not the last one, I amend as I catch sight of Ryan Hunter coming down the walking path that winds from Damien's Malibu house all the way to the beach where I'm now standing. Ryan is the Chief of Security for Stark International, and he and I have been the *de facto* host and hostess for this post-wedding soiree ever since the bride and groom took off in a helicopter bound for marital bliss.

Ryan is not among the eighty-percent, and that is truly a shame. The man is seriously hot, with piercing blue eyes and chestnut hair worn in a short, almost military style that accents the hard lines and angles of his face. He's tall and lean, but strong and sexy. I've seen him now in both jeans and a tux, and the curve of his ass alone is enough to make a woman drool.

We've gotten to know each other over the last few months, and I consider him a friend. Frankly, I'd like to consider him more, and I think he feels the same, even though he has yet to make a move.

I've seen the way he watches me, the heat that flares in his eyes when he thinks I'm not looking. Maybe he's shy—but I doubt it. He's got a dangerous edge that perfectly suits his job as the head security dude for a guy like Damien and an enterprise like Stark International.

Nikki once told me that there was nothing Ryan liked better than chasing monsters. I believe it, and as I watch him stride down the walking path, his movements a combination of grace and power, I can imagine him in battle and am certain that he would do whatever it takes to win.

No, I don't believe that Ryan Hunter is shy. All I know is that he's never made a move on me, and that's a damn shame.

And now, of course, it's too late. Because I'm heading back home to Texas tomorrow as part of my newly implemented life goal of getting my shit together. And, as part of the whole Repair My Life plan, I've put the kibosh on sleeping around. I'm focusing on Jamie Archer. On figuring out who she is and what she wants, and step one of The Plan is to not do the nasty with every hot guy who crosses my path.

Honestly, men are so five minutes ago.

So far, The Plan is going pretty good. I found a tenant for my Studio City condo a few months ago, then went home to live with my parents in Dallas. It's hard being a twenty-five-year-old actress in Los Angeles, especially one who has yet to land a decent gig. There are too many guys who are prettier than me—and who know it. And way too many opportunities for a fast fuck.

Texas is slower. Easier. And even though it's hardly the acting capital of the universe, I've already had a few auditions, and I think I may even have a decent shot for a job as an on-air reporter at a local affiliate. I'd auditioned right before flying out here for the wedding, and I'm hoping to hear back from the programming director any day now.

And, yes, true, I'd also auditioned for a commercial here in SoCal, but I didn't get the job. I tell myself that's a good thing because I would have taken it and stayed in Los Angeles, because I love Los Angeles and my friends are here. But that would have put me right back on that hamster wheel of auditioning and fucking, and then starting the whole destructive process right over again.

The Plan is good, I tell myself as I watch the crew finish the job. The Plan is wise.

As a dozen workmen haul the last of the tent poles to a nearby truck, the supervisor approaches me with a clipboard and a pen. He takes me through the list, and I duly check off all the various items, confirming that the final details have been attended to.

Then I sign the form, thank him, and watch as he climbs into the truck and drives away.

"So that's it," Ryan says as he approaches me. He's still in tuxedo pants and the starched white shirt, but the cummerbund is gone, as is the jacket. He really does look sexy as hell, but it's his bare feet that have done me in. There's something so damn devil-may-care about a guy in a tux barefoot on the beach, and I can't help but wonder if there really is a bit of the devil in Ryan Hunter.

And if there is, will I ever get to peek at the wickedness?

"No more cars in the driveway," he continues, as I try to yank my thoughts back to reality. "And I just signed the invoice for the car park company. I think we can safely call this thing a wrap. And a success." His smile is slow and easy and undeniably sexy. "It really was one hell of a party."

I laugh. "I was just thinking the same thing." My stomach does a little twisting number, and I tell myself it's hunger. After all, champagne isn't that filling, and I'm sure all the dancing I did during the night burned off the three slices of wedding cake I'd devoured.

I'm lying again, of course. It's not hunger that's making my stomach flutter. It's Ryan. And as I stand there silently wishing he'd just touch me already, I'm also getting more and more irritated. Because why the hell *hasn't* he touched me already? We've spent time together. We've even danced together during various club outings with friends. Not touching, maybe, but close enough that the air between us was thick with promise.

And once, when Damien had a security scare, he sent Ryan to check on me. I'd been wearing a tiny bikini with a sheer cover-up, and I looked damn hot. But he hadn't made a move. We'd ended up talking for hours, which was great, and I even made him eggs, which is about as domesticated as I get.

I'm certain I haven't been imagining that sizzle between us—and yet never once has he made a move. I can't fathom why, and the whole situation grates on me.

Except I'm not supposed to care—Ryan is not part of The Plan.

He starts to walk toward the surf, and I fall in step beside him. I'd kicked off my own shoes once the workmen hauled away the dance floor because beaches and two-inch heels really don't go well together, and the sand beneath my feet feels amazing.

I love strolling the beach in the morning. There's so much to look at—the seagulls that scavenge for their breakfast, the waves that pour like latte foam onto the sand, the tanned hard bodies of twenty-something surfer dudes out to catch a morning swell. It's like a little slice of heaven.

This morning, Ryan adds value to the view. His sleeves are rolled up, revealing well-muscled forearms, and when he bends down to pick up a lovely purple seashell, I find myself fascinated by his hands. They're large and strong, but as they hold the shell, I can't help but think that his touch would be surprisingly gentle.

I start to pick up my pace because, hello, mind really not supposed to be going there, but he reaches for me, holding the shell in his outstretched hand. "A souvenir," he says, and though his smile is casual, there's nothing easy about the heat in his eyes. His gaze is hot enough to cut right through me. The hair at the back of my neck prickles, and for a moment, I'm not certain I remember how to breathe. "I'd hate for you to get back to Texas and forget everything you've left behind."

"Oh." My voice sounds breathy, and I take the shell, my fingers brushing his palm as I do. I feel the shock of contact all the way down to my toes, and I expect him to pull me close. To touch me. To do some damn thing so that I'm not just standing there feeling all hot and horny.

He does nothing—and the sharp prick of irritation breaks through the wall of lust. I close my hand around the shell and force myself to aim an equally casual smile back at him. "Thanks."

I'm grateful my voice sounds normal despite the fact that I am both genuinely moved and undeniably irritated. Moved because it's a lovely shell and the gesture is very sweet. Irritated because now I'm getting mixed signals from a hot guy who still hasn't touched me and who I have absolutely no business being interested in.

My libido, however, still hasn't gotten the message because there's some serious sizzle and pop going on. To be honest, there's been sizzle and pop since the first time I met Ryan.

Down girl.

I take a deep breath and mentally recite what has now become a mantra: *Plan. Texas. New leaf. New Jamie.*

I start walking again because he's made me too antsy to just stand still. "Are you flying back today?" he asks, falling easily into step with me.

"Not flying. Driving." I see the confusion on his face—Nikki had been stuck in a meeting and had asked Ryan to pick me up at the airport just over a week ago. Yet another encounter where I felt both sizzle and pop—but he didn't touch me once.

Honestly, I need to stop this mental tally; I'm going to give myself a complex.

"Planning on doing a little recreational car shopping today?"

"Nikki and Damien gave me a car for my birthday," I mumble, because I'm still a bit embarrassed by such an extravagant gift. Not that it's extravagant to a guy like Damien. I'm pretty sure that to him, Australia wouldn't be too much.

"Happy birthday," Ryan says in the kind of voice that makes me think that he would make a damn good present. Especially with a big red bow in just the right place.

I clear my throat, banishing the thought. "Right. Yeah, well, it's not really my birthday. They were planning on just giving it to me because, you know, my Corolla has seen better days. And I said I couldn't accept it, and Nikki said..." I trail off, shrugging.

"She's a good friend." He's walking in the surf now, the waves breaking around his feet.

"Cold." I say, nodding toward his feet.

"A little." He tilts his head up, his gaze taking me in before he finally meets my eyes. "But I'm willing to put up with all sorts of things if it gets me something I want."

Wow. "Right." I swallow, then curl my hands into fists so that I don't lean in, grab his collar, and kiss him. "Um. So. What is it you want?"

"To walk on the beach with you, of course."

And there it is. That *pow*, that *snap*. He takes my hand, the gesture light and casual. Seemingly friendly, but really it's so much more.

He's intense, I think. *Strong. Silent. Steady.* The kind of guy who knows what he wants and goes after it methodically and relentlessly.

Is he going after me? I shiver a little as I slide into a nice little *From Here to Eternity* fantasy. Not that I've ever actually watched the movie, but I've seen that famous sex in the surf scene, and I'm more than happy to let my imagination fill in the blanks.

"You're not driving back to Texas today, are you?" He is watching me closely, his eyes as deep and intense as the Pacific behind us. "You were up all night. You shouldn't risk it."

"I'm not," I say, imagining the surf crashing over me and Ryan's body hot above me. "I'm staying the night and heading out first thing tomorrow."

"I'm very glad to hear it." His voice is as smooth as whiskey, and I wonder if I'm getting a little bit drunk on it. "I'd worry about you."

I stand there, feeling nine kinds of itchy, and wait for him to make a move. But the move doesn't come.

I tell myself that's a good thing.

Then I tell myself I'm a goddamn liar.

Then I remind myself about The Plan.

But you know what? Screw The Plan. The Plan is for Texas, after all. I mean, I've pretty much already established that when in California, Jamie Archer is a hot mess. So why not be a mess one last time with this incredibly sexy guy who is making me tingle?

Except that doesn't seem to be an option.

Because Ryan isn't making a move. I consider making a pass myself. After all, I've never once been shy about going after a guy I wanted in my bed. With Ryan, though, I can't seem to take that first step, and it's weird. I'm feeling shy and awkward, and I am never shy or awkward.

Maybe it's the lingering effect of The Plan. Residual guilt. Pre-justification. My subconscious telling me that if he pursues me, then a California fuck is okay. But me going after him is totally against the rules.

All of which is a load of twisted and convoluted bullshit, but I never said my subconscious was a linear thinker.

Just go for it.

Holy crap, this shouldn't be that difficult. I mean, honestly. When I decided to bang Kevin in 2H, I cornered him in the laundry room, put my hand on his crotch, and asked him if he wanted to fuck. So why the hell am I all sixth-grade girl with a crush where Ryan Hunter is concerned?

Right. Okay. Diving in now...

I clear my throat. "So here's the thing," I say, and I don't get any further. Maybe, I think, he'll pick up the thread.

He doesn't. He just looks at me, all innocent interest and calm curiosity. His expression is bland, and yet I have the distinct impression that he's amused.

"It's just that I can't figure you out," I blurt.

"Can't you?"

"We've had some good times, right? And I've seen you look at me." I lick my lips, hating how nervous I feel. "And I know

I've looked at you. So what's the deal?"

"The deal?"

I tilt my head a little and give him my best seductive smile. "You've never made a pass at me," I say in the kind of voice that makes clear I would be very receptive to one right now.

"No," he says, "I haven't."

"Oh." I mentally backpedal. That wasn't the response I was expecting. "Okay. So, why not? You're just not interested?"

"On the contrary. Maybe I assumed you weren't interested."

"Seriously?"

"I've had my eye on you for a while, Ms. Archer. And as far as I've seen, you're not the least bit shy about making a move on a man you want."

I hear the raw heat in his voice, but I can't tell if he is serious or if he's playing me. All I know is that the more he looks at me with those fathomless blue eyes and the more he speaks to me in that musically sexy voice, the more I melt, until I fear that I'll dissolve right there and be washed away when the tide comes in.

"Oh," I say stupidly. Dear god I want him to touch me. I've slept with a lot of guys, but right now, I don't think I've ever been more desperate for a man's touch.

I think about The Plan. I think about my loophole.

I think about the fact that the loophole calls for him to make a move on me.

And then I think, *what the hell. Just go for it.*

"All right," I say as I quash those damn nerves, then fist my hand in his shirt and move in close. He smells like musk and desire and I breathe deep, letting the scent of him fill me, warm me. We're not even inches apart, and the air between us seems to shimmer, thick with passion.

I press my other hand to his thigh and stroke slowly up, up, up, until I brush against the hard length of his erection. My thighs quiver, and my sex tightens with need. I'm aware of every inch of my body, as if I'm a live wire, sparking and popping.

We're well-matched in height, and I only have to rise up a little on my toes in order to claim his mouth with mine. I close my hand over the steel of his cock and feel it twitch under my touch. I hear his moan, and it only makes me wetter.

His hands twine in my hair, pulling me closer as he deepens the kiss, fucking me with his mouth, going deep, making me wet, so incredibly wet, so that all I want is to slide my hand into his trousers and free him, then fall onto the sand, yank my dress up, and scream as he fucks me harder than I've ever been fucked in my life.

I am gasping when he breaks the kiss. I'm alive with need, my breasts aching for his touch, my cunt throbbing with demand. I'm wild, desperate, and when I see the matching wildness in his eyes, I know that this is going to be one hell of an amazing morning.

"All right," I say again, my voice breathless and heavy with longing. "That was me, making a move."

"And this," he says gently as he takes a single step away from me, "is me, saying no."

Chapter Two

"No," I say into the phone. "The bastard actually said no."

I'm in the guest suite that has become my temporary home. I have my headphones in, and am spread out on the bed, idly petting Lady Meow Meow as I stare out through the French doors toward the pristine beach upon which I was so soundly spurned. "I mean, can you believe it? He turned me down flat."

From somewhere in Mexico, Nikki's voice filters over the line. "Actually, I can't believe it. I've seen the way he looks at you, and there is some serious lust happening. But, James, what the hell were you doing coming on to him in the first place? I thought you were doing a moratorium on sex."

Since I really don't want to get in to my convoluted logic with my best friend, I fall back on reason and rationality. "You know what? I'm an idiot. I can't believe I dumped all that on you. And what the hell are you doing calling me anyway? Aren't you supposed to be banging Damien's brains out?"

"Did that," she says with the kind of sigh that makes me jealous. "And I expect a repeat performance very soon. But right now he's on the phone, too. We're flying to Paris tonight and he's checking in with the pilot. And since I didn't have the chance to tell you good-bye before the honeymoon, I wanted to call. I love you, you know. And I'm so glad you were my maid of honor. Also, Damien wanted me to remind you that the gas gauge on the Ferrari isn't working. He's going to e-mail you where to take it when you get to Dallas, but in the meantime, pay attention to the odometer and get gas when you've burned about half a tank, okay?"

"I know. He already told me at least a dozen times." The car that Damien and Nikki gave me is the same sleek, sexy Ferrari that I accidentally totaled in San Bernardino. At least, I'd thought I'd totaled it. Apparently Damien called in the best car surgeons in the world and got her up and running again. And then—to my shock and amazement—he and Nikki gave the Ferrari to me. "I still can't believe that you guys—"

"Will you shut up about it, already? You love the car. We love you. End of story."

"Right. Thanks." I can practically hear Nikki rolling her eyes, and the thought makes me grin. "Right," I say again, then clear my throat. "So what should I do about Ryan?"

She sighs. "Hell, James, I wish I knew what to tell you. I like Ryan—I like him a lot, actually. And if you weren't—" She cuts herself off. "You know what? Never mind."

"Oh, no," I say. "You are so not getting away with that. Whatever you were going to say, just say it. I already know I'm a head case, so it's not like you'll be telling me something I don't already know."

"Jamie." Her voice is soft and a little sad. "I just worry about you, that's all."

I shift my position on the bed, feeling vaguely uncomfortable. "I know you do," I say as the cat gets up, yawns, and then pads out of the room, apparently uninterested in my drama. "Just like I worry about you. But you've got Damien for that now."

"Doesn't mean I don't need my best friend," she says, and I must be more fragile than I thought because a tear escapes and trickles down my cheek.

"Listen," she says gently. "We both know what a mess I am, but I'm not the only one with scars, and I worry about you. I like Ryan," she says again. "But I don't want you getting hurt. For that matter, I don't want you hurting him."

"Not a problem on either count," I say. "In case you missed the major talking point of this conversation, he blew me off."

"Just don't push it, okay. Go home. Get your head on straight. Don't—"

"Don't what?"

"Don't go after him like sex is a weapon or something. Promise me."

"I won't," I say. "It's not." I'm not lying—I've never used sex as a weapon, not really. Instead, I've used it as a shield. Keep the control, keep the guys on a leash. Keep it fun, keep it play. Never serious. Never deep.

Because if you don't let them past the barrier, they can't break your heart.

"I love you," Nikki says, and in those three little words, I hear perfect understanding.

"I know," I say. "And I swear I'm not going to do anything except go home to Dallas. So I don't need the lecture or the reminder or whatever you want to call it. Really. Now go be married or something."

"That," she says, "is a great idea." I laugh, then give her a quick rundown on what happened on the beach after she and Damien left, and she promises to text me from Paris so I'll know they arrived safe and sound. I tell her not to bother. I've already seen their wedding photos on Twitter. I'm sure the paparazzi in Paris will be tweeting, too.

And then the call is over and I'm left lying on the bed looking out at that damn beach and wondering why the hell Ryan walked way.

Yes, I am just that pathetic.

I sit up, annoyed with myself. It's over. It's done. Ryan's long gone—I'd stood on the beach and watched as he walked back to the house. I hadn't wanted to follow. Call it embarrassment or pride, but I hung out for at least an hour before I finally dragged my ass back to the house, every step requiring a major effort.

Funny, despite working so hard yesterday to pull the party together—and then dancing and partying and drinking through the night—I hadn't felt tired before. Certainly not when Ryan had showed up and walked me down the beach, or when he'd leaned in close, or when he'd set my body to tingle.

On the contrary, just being near him was like sucking down an energy drink, leaving me breathless and recharged and just a little edgy.

Or it had felt that way until he'd gone. Now I want to crash. I'm bone tired and lost and, although I was so glad to have heard from Nikki, I'm now feeling more than a little melancholy. And very much alone.

When I'd first returned to the house, I'd thought I would see him. But the house was empty and silent, and though I checked the front drive, there was no sign of a car, and I'd gone back inside and stomped my way to my guest suite feeling both relieved and annoyed. Relieved, because I apparently made a fool of myself earlier. Annoyed because as far as the wedding went, Ryan and I had the joint responsibility of dealing with the reception and the house guests. We'd been working closely for almost forty-eight hours now, and at the very least he should have checked with me before leaving to make sure there wasn't anything still to do.

There isn't. But he should have checked.

I tell myself I don't care, and I'm just feeling touchy because I'm exhausted. I need a nap. Some R&R. I'll lay out by the pool, then take a swim. Maybe this afternoon I'll go into town and prowl the little shops. I should take something fun back to my parents—maybe a painting for the entryway or something cute for the kitchen.

Then I'll grab some takeout and crash for the night. I'll get a good night's sleep, get in the car, and get my ass back to Texas. Away from California, temptation, and Ryan Fucking Hunter.

It's a good plan, and I go to change into my bathing suit and find something to read. I recently started to reread *Rebecca*, but right now I'm not in the mood. Instead I grab a copy of *Cosmopolitan*. I smile wryly. Maybe this month's article on how to make a man feel awesome in bed will come in handy if I ever see Ryan again.

As with everything in this house that Damien built, the backyard pool area is a little slice of heaven. The pool itself is huge, falling off to an infinity edge that gives the illusion that it extends into the Pacific. There's a hot tub, of course, as well as a waterfall and a swim-up bar.

The water is warm—and it feels nice to walk in until it hits my shoulders. Then I close my eyes and sink under, losing myself to the eerie quiet of this empty pool.

I'm not in the mood to swim, though, and so I emerge, then lightly towel off. I like the sensation of being damp, of lying back and feeling the breeze brushing over my moist skin.

The lounge chair is padded, with a nice cup holder built right in. And since I'm planning on napping anyway, I detour to the small refrigerator and take out a wine cooler. I pick a chair under the pergola so that I'm at least a little bit out of the sun. And then, finally, I settle down to read and relax.

I make it only a few pages into the magazine before my eyes start to droop. I drop the magazine to the tiled decking, then close my eyes. Just a short nap, I think, as sleep beckons and I'm pulled down, down, down into my dreams.

He is there.

Ryan.

I am standing in a wide green field, and though I cannot see him clearly, I know that he is the man in the distance. *Hunter*, I think. *And I am his prey.*

He stalks toward me, jeans slung low on his hips. He wears no shirt, and the sun beats down on broad shoulders and a lean, sculptured chest. I move toward him, drawn to him by some unassailable compulsion.

And then he is there, and we are no longer in a field but on a beach. I am in his arms and there is an orchestra, and Nikki is there with Damien, applauding as Ryan spins me around and around and around until I am so dizzy I need to lie down.

Then I am on the ground, and the waves crash over me. The tent is gone, the orchestra vanished. There is only the sound of the ocean crashing upon the beach. There is only the feel of the water sluicing over me.

It is not cold—instead it is warm, so warm. And I stretch, feeling soft and languid and needful—I want his hands, his touch. And then, in the way of dreams, he is there, his hard body over me, his mouth trailing up my calf, my thigh.

I shiver, realizing that I am naked, but there is no shyness. I spread my legs for him and arch back as his mouth closes over my cunt. He kisses me there, so deeply intimate that shocks of pleasure ricochet through me. His tongue plays me, laving me, then teasing my clit, bringing me so very, very close before he torments me even more by trailing those kisses up my abdomen.

His hands massage my breasts roughly, his fingers pinching my nipples, sending live wires of electricity all the way down to my sex. My cunt clenches, desperate with the need to have him inside me, and I moan in an incoherent demand for more.

Then his mouth closes over mine, silencing me, and I taste him—taste me. I feel his erection hard beneath my legs, the steel length of him rubbing provocatively against my sex.

I moan against his mouth, and he gently pulls away. The shock of the break tugs me toward wakefulness. "Do you want me inside you?" he whispers, his voice still filling my dreams. "Do you want me to fuck you?"

"Yes," I murmur, even as sleep abandons me. "Oh, yes."

I am awake now but somehow still trapped in the dream. My

cunt is slick with need, and the way the sun beats down on me makes me feel loose and sensual.

Slowly, as if in a dream, I skim one hand down my body. I am wearing a tiny bikini, and as I brush my fingers over my breast, I gasp from the contact with my too-sensitive nipples. Then I continue south, my palm flat on my stomach, my muscles quivering, as I move so painfully slowly down my belly.

He is still in my head. Hunter, I think. I like it. It seems wild. Hot. Hunter wouldn't have walked away. Hunter would have thrown me back on the beach and fucked me right there, and not cared in the slightest if anyone walked by.

The thought makes me a little crazy, and I squeeze my legs together even as I wiggle my hips. The motion takes some of the edge off, but not enough. I need more. I need Ryan, the fantasy.

I raise one hand to my chest and slide my fingers under the bikini top and over the swell of my breast until I brush against my nipple. The sensation is delicious, and I arch a bit under my own touch. My breasts feel heavy, my nipples straining against the thin triangles of material that form the top.

I stroke my nipple, teasing it even as my first hand sinks lower and lower, until those fingers sneak in beneath the elastic band at the top of the bikini bottoms. Then I slide them further still, until I find my own slick heat. I gasp, arching up at the sweet jolt that shoots through me when I lightly stroke my clit.

I'm desperately wet, frantically wanting. But it's not just release that I want, it's the man.

There's no denying it—I want Ryan Hunter. And if I can't have the man himself, I'm going to have him in my imagination.

I move my finger in small, teasing circles, letting the pleasure build, arching up to bring it tighter, hotter.

I bite my lower lip and squeeze my eyes shut as I slide two fingers into my sex, then arch up as my body clenches tight with unfulfilled need. I quiver, arching, moving, trying desperately to reach satisfaction.

I tug the bikini top down, freeing my breasts, and gasp at the sensation of warm sun upon my nipples. I take one between two fingers and pinch, crying out as heat shoots all the way down to my overly sensitive clit.

I withdraw my hand and stroke an ever-quickening circle on my sensitive sex, but it's not enough. I want to be claimed, taken. I want to feel his cock inside me, not just his hands upon me. And I abandon my aching and heavy breasts to slide that hand down, lower and lower until I am gasping with the pleasure of having two fingers stroke my clit while I fuck myself with my other hand.

No. Not myself.

Hunter.

"Yes," I murmur, not even certain if I'm speaking aloud. "Oh, god, yes."

In my mind, I can see him above me, his eyes searching mine. I can hear his voice, telling me to come for him, to explode with him. It is his cock in me, thrusting deeper and harder, taking me. Claiming me. Owning me.

"Hunter," I cry as my eyes flutter open while his fingers—my fingers—thrust even deeper inside me.

And there he is.

I go tense, frozen, as Ryan Hunter stands there watching me—with a heat in his eyes so intense it is a wonder I don't get burned.

Chapter Three

I start to yank my hand away and am rendered frozen by his sharp, firm, "*No.*"

My heart is beating. My skin is flushed. I'm embarrassed and turned on and confused. "Ryan," I say. "I—what are you—"

I start to shift. I need to move. Hell, I need to run.

"No," he says more softly this time, but the word is equally firm, and the force of it holds me in place. "Don't stop. Come for me, Jamie. I want to watch you explode for me."

I am tempted to tell him to go to hell. To wrap a towel around myself and run inside.

I'm tempted to do that—but only because I think that is what I should do. But I've never been a girl who pays attention to *should*. I'm all about *want*.

And what I want is to finish this.

What I want is to make him hard, to drive him crazy. And I know that he is close. I can see the evidence even from this distance. The bulge in his jeans. The tightness in his jaw. The way his hand is closed tight around the decorative finial on the gate by which he stands.

He is as turned on as I am, and that knowledge makes me bold.

He'd driven me a little crazy when he'd left me on the beach. And now, I think, as I run my teeth over my lower lip and slide my finger over my swollen clit—now it's my turn to drive him wild.

And that's a game I've been playing for years.

I don't speak. Instead, I keep my eyes on him as I slide my hand further down. I'm wet and slick, and the tension I see on his face only excites me more.

I thrust my fingers inside, my hips bucking as I finger fuck myself with him watching, him wanting.

I slide my fingers in and out, teasing myself by rubbing lightly over my clit. I keep up the motion, my eyes on Ryan, my mouth open and my breath coming hard.

I draw my other hand up to fondle my breast, and as I do, I hear him suck in air. The sound only turns me on more, and I start to close my eyes as the tension inside me builds, higher and higher.

"No," he says. "I want to see your eyes. I want to look at you when you come."

I open my eyes and our gazes lock. He is heat. He is power.

He is everything I want, and I am starting to wonder if I will be able to survive this. If I will be able to withstand the force of the explosion that is building inside me.

"That's it," he says. "You're close. Christ, Jamie, do you have any idea how hard I am? How much I want to be inside you?"

I thrust my fingers into my cunt and slide my other hand down, my hips bucking violently. I am wild. I am shameless, and my eyes never leave his. Not as the tension starts to build. Not as the sparks start to gather. Not as the electricity surges through me, building and building until there is nowhere left to go, and I cry out because there is no way I could keep that much passion inside.

I hold his gaze as my body shudders, as the tremors calm and I return to earth.

I watch his eyes and think that for the first time, someone has seen into the heart of me.

I lie there, my breathing shallow, as Ryan strides toward me, all power and purpose. His expression is hard, his eyes blazing. My lips are parted, and I arch my back without thinking, bringing my body that much closer to him in a silent plea for his touch.

He doesn't reach for me, though. Instead, he stops beside the chaise and looks down at me. His gaze moves slowly over me with such sweet deliberation that I tremble, my body quivering as if in reaction to his touch.

"Tell me," he says. "Tell me who you were thinking of."

"No one," I say though I know he will see through the lie.

"Don't lie to me, kitten. I don't like it."

I lick my lips. "I had you wrong," I tease. "I thought you were a nice guy. I made you eggs one morning, remember? I never thought that the nice guy I shared breakfast with would have—"

"Would have what?"

"Would have watched me finger fuck myself," I finish boldly.

"Watch?" he repeats as he lowers himself to sit on the edge of my chaise. His hip brushes the bare skin of my waist, making me hyperaware of his proximity. "I did more than watch, sweetheart." He lifts my hand, then strokes it slowly, making me even more crazy in the process.

"I imagined that these fingers were mine. That it was me stroking your skin, sliding under your suit." He moves my hand to my belly as he speaks, then he places his own hand flat on the back of mine before easing our joined hands down.

"Do you have any idea how hard I got imagining how slick you were, how tight your cunt was?" He guides two of my fingers inside me, and I gasp in pleasure and surprise as he pushes them deeper and deeper.

"Please," I beg, but I don't even know what I am asking for. I am a wild mess of feelings, hot and out of control. I want to come. I want to explode. I want his hands all over me.

"That's it," he says as I thrust my hips shamelessly, wanting more. Wanting everything. "Oh, yes. You like that, don't you, kitten?"

"Yes," I whisper. "God yes." And yet I don't know this woman—this girl who melts at a man's voice, who submits to his whims. The Jamie I know keeps control by keeping a tight grip on a man's cock and leading him around with it like a leash. But this Jamie—oh, dear god, right then all this Jamie wants to do is surrender to pleasure.

He is only tormenting me, though, a sad fact I realize when he withdraws my fingers, then tugs our joined hands free. Then he raises my hand to his lips, and I begin to melt again as he draws my finger in, sucking and licking with such deliberate intensity that I can feel the tug of pressure all the way down to my clit.

"Am I a nice guy?" he asks as he releases my hand. "I don't know, Jamie. I guess that's up to you. If you need a nice guy, I'll be a nice guy. But I don't think that's what you need right now."

I try to speak, but can't seem to manage. I swallow, then try again. "What do I need?"

But he says nothing. He just smiles. And, honestly, he's turned me into such a confused and emotional mess that I'm not sure if I want to kiss him or slap him.

I don't like being confused, and my discomfort makes me bold. I prop myself up on my elbows. "What the hell kind of a game are you playing?"

"Who says I'm playing a game?"

"I do."

He cocks his head. "All right. Why?"

"I seem to recall you saying no to me on the beach. And yet here you are."

"Yes," he says. "Here I am."

"Ryan."

He shakes his head, then strokes a finger along the line of my jaw. It's a familiar, almost sweet gesture, and it unnerves me. "You called me Hunter before you knew I was watching. I liked it."

"Ryan," I say again firmly. "What's your fucking game?"

He looks at me for so long I start to wonder if I should just call it a wrap and go inside. "Do you know why I said no?" he finally says.

I shake my head.

"Because I've watched you, Jamie. Watched and wanted. I want to kiss you, to touch you. I want to fuck you, Jamie, but I want so much more than that, too."

"What?" I ask, mesmerized by his words.

"Everything," he says simply. "I want to tie you up and fuck you until you beg for mercy. I want to use my palm to redden that ass—because we both know how naughty you've been. I want to make you come so fast and so hard that you scream, and then do it all over again."

I lick my lips, my body already tingling in anticipation.

"In other words," he continues, "I want you at my mercy, kitten. And I intend to make you purr."

"Kitten?" I repeat. "Are you trying to tame me?"

"On the contrary. I like you wild. But I won't have you walk," he says firmly. "I won't be one of the men you toss aside."

He looks at me, and his expression is hard. This is the man who runs security for a multi-billion dollar corporation; this is a man who gets what he wants.

"So you tell me, Jamie," he says. "Do you want me to fuck you? Or should I walk away right now?"

Chapter Four

Every ounce of self-preservation tells me to play it coy. To insist that I don't do ultimatums. To tell him that I know damn well he wants me as much as I want him.

In other words, to take back the power.

I don't.

I can't take the risk that he will call my bluff. That he'll walk away.

Because, damn me, I want the man.

I know all the reasons that I should tell him no—but I also know that I won't.

Because right here, right now, I want this man inside me more than I have ever wanted any man. Hell, more than I've ever wanted anything.

"Jamie," he says. "What do you want?"

"Yes," I whisper.

"Yes, what?"

Slowly, I stand. Then I tilt my head so that I can look at him more directly. "Yes, everything," I say. "You want me at your mercy? I'm already there."

Pure desire cuts across his face, and I press my hand against his chest, then slide it down over his slick, hard chest. "Fuck me, Ryan Hunter. I want you to fuck me right now."

"Well," he says as he reaches behind me to unhook the back of my bikini top, "I do like the sound of that."

The top hangs loose, and as he steps closer—as he reaches behind me to slowly lift my shoulder-length hair and then tug the bow at my neck free—I try to breathe, but seem to have forgotten how.

The top falls off my body, and I tilt my gaze down to see it land at my feet. I look back up to meet Ryan's eyes. They are blue flames and seem ready to burn.

"The bottoms," he says in a voice so tight with want that it does not sound like him. "Take them off."

I swallow, then slowly ease my hands down my hips, hooking my fingers under the material, then shimmying out of the tiny bottoms. I let them fall to my ankles, then step out. I'm breathing hard, hyperaware of every tiny hair on my body. Of every small bead of sweat at the back of my neck. My nipples are hard and my areolae puckered. I am wet, and because I am waxed, I know that he can see how hot and swollen and ready I am.

He lowers his eyes to my feet, then traces his gaze slowly up my body. I try to stand still, but it is as if his inspection is a caress, and when he lingers at my sex—when he releases a low groan full of pleasure and need—it is all I can do not to slide my hand between my legs and try to release some of this building pressure.

His gaze continues up, lingering over my breasts before

settling on my face. "You are stunning," he says. "I like seeing you aroused. It makes the fire in you burn hotter."

"You do that," I say.

"I like that, too," he retorts.

I lick my lips, waiting for him to tell me what to do, but he says nothing. I try to withstand the silence, but it is impossible. "Please," I say.

"Please what?"

"Please touch me."

He cocks his head as if considering the idea, then nods once. "Lay down on the chaise," he says, and when I go there, he shakes his head. "No. Face down. And keep your legs apart," he orders. "I want to see how wet you are. How much you want me."

"Very much," I admit as I move to comply.

I have laid out naked many times before, even here at this house when it was only me and Nikki looking to work on our tans. But I never thought of it as sexual. It was just me. Just skin.

Now, even the sensation of the sun on my lower back is erotic, and when Ryan steps to my side and then traces a finger lightly from my heel, up my calf and thigh, then over the curve of my ass and all the way to my shoulder, I fear that I just may die from the pleasure. "Wait here. Don't move."

I do as he says, though I cheat a little by spreading my legs more. I want him to see me—I want him to want me. And more than that, I want the sensation of the sun between my legs. Heat upon heat, fire added to fire.

He comes back quickly and without explanation, but when he sits beside me, I see that he has brought suntan oil. He squirts some onto my back, making me twitch from the sudden, ticklish sensation. But that is quickly quelled when his hands begin to stroke me, long, slow movements that heat my skin and fill the air with the scent of coconut and vanilla.

He pampers every inch of me, working on my hands—stroking and pulling each finger in a manner so erotic that every caress is reflected in my sex, which throbs and wants more and more as each moment passes.

He strokes my shoulders in deep, soothing motions, then moves down to knead my waist, my hips, and even my ass. He doesn't slip further down, though—doesn't touch me where I am so desperate to be touched. Instead he moves lower still, making my thighs slick, then focusing on my calves, my heels, the arch of my foot.

My breathing is fast, shallow. I squirm, silently begging him to slide his slick, oiled hand between my legs. But he is deliberate in his torment and does not take the hint. Instead, he bends low, brushing his lips against my ear and softly telling me to turn over.

I do, then force myself not to arch up in pleasure and longing as he gently but firmly rubs the oil over my breasts, then down my abdomen to stroke lazily over my pubis.

"I like that you're waxed," he says. "I like seeing your skin. Seeing you flush. Seeing how aroused and swollen you are. I bet you feel slick on my tongue. And now," he adds as he slides his oil-slick hand between my legs, "I bet you taste like coconut."

"Why don't you find out?" I ask, my words little more than breaths.

"Maybe I will," he says, then moves to the end of the chaise, roughly thrusts my legs apart, and buries his mouth between my legs, his tongue thrusting deep inside me.

The shift from slow and lazy to hard and wild is so unexpected that I arch up in surprise, lost in the swell of pleasure that is growing deeper and wilder within me.

"Yes," I murmur, squirming against him, wanting him deeper in me, sucking me off, taking me all the way. "Yes, Hunter, oh, damn, yes."

But then, just as I am about to explode, he draws away, leaving a soft trail of kisses descending down my inner thigh.

"No," I protest. "Please don't stop."

"I'm not going to stop, kitten. I intend to have you every way I can, and then some. Sit up now," he orders, and when I comply, he peels off his clothes.

I watch, mesmerized as he steps out of the briefs that are straining to hold in his erection. He is long and thick and perfect, and I lick my lips out of reflex. He notices and raises a brow. "Interesting," he says. "Do you want to suck my cock."

My own sex clenches with desire at those bold, simple words. "Yes," I say, imagining the feel of him, the taste of him. Imagining even more the way his body would tighten and tremble, done in by my power to take him to the edge.

"Good," he says. "But I have other plans at the moment." He sits on the edge of the chaise. "Come here. Now turn around," he says when I arrive facing him. I turn, and in my peripheral vision, I see him reach down and grab a condom packet. He rolls it on, then takes my hips and eases me backward.

"Knees on the chaise," he says. "Kneel over me."

I glance backward, then do as he says. It's awkward getting on the chaise, then straddling him. But his hands are firm at my hips, and once I'm over him, I feel the head of his cock thrusting against me, and I wriggle, wanting him inside me.

"Go ahead," Ryan says. "Take me. Take all of me."

I reach between us and guide his cock into me, then I lower myself. He feels incredible, and I rise and fall, levering with my knees, up and down on his shaft. He is thick inside me, and the pleasure of this position is only enhanced when he lets go of one hip and slides his hand around to play with my clit.

Tremors run though my body, and I rock faster and faster. My hands go to my breasts, and then, when he takes his hand away from my clit, I cry out in protest, because I so desperately want to come with him.

"It's okay. Touch yourself," he says, and as he speaks, I feel his finger stroke me from behind, teasing my ass even as my finger plays with my clit and his cock fills me.

I am overwhelmed. I am nothing but pleasure and sensation and raw, wild need.

"Hunter," I cry, as I piston faster against him, as the pressure builds inside me, as I feel him tremble deep, deep within. "Hunter." I scream his name, and as I do, the world explodes around us and he empties himself inside me.

I collapse back against him, and he pulls me tight, his hands cupping my breasts, stroking and soothing. "That's it, kitten. God, yes, that was perfect."

We sit that way for a moment, and then he slowly lowers us both, our bodies still connected, to the chaise. I am breathing hard, feeling decadent and satisfied and wanton. He is gently kissing my back, my shoulders, and I think that for this moment, I have found heaven.

"I'm not done with you yet," he murmurs, just as I am about to drift off to sleep. Instantly, I am awake again.

"No?"

"Oh, no," he says. "I have plans for you. For that cunt. For that mouth." He pulls out, semi-soft now, and rolls over to face me. "But only if you want more. I could have you all day and all night, so if you want to stop, you need to be the one to tell me."

"No," I whisper. "Don't stop. Please. Don't ever stop."

"You're staying in the guest suite?"

I nod.

"Go there. Wait for me."

I do, padding barefoot and naked to the room that is my home whenever I stay in this house. I have never been uncomfortable in this room, but I am now. I don't know where to sit or what to do. I don't know how he wants me. I only know that I want to please him because I do not want this to end.

I feel wilder than I have ever felt with any man, and I want to go further with him than I have with any man. That makes me vulnerable, and that's not something that I'm used to.

With Hunter, though, I like it.

Finally, I lay on the bed. I want him to see how much I need him. How turned on I am. I spread my legs and slide my hand over my sex. Then I close my eyes and imagine it is him.

"Now that is a pretty picture," he says when he enters the room only minutes later. He is still naked, but now he has a length of cord coiled around his shoulder. In his hand, he holds a single glass of wine.

I try not to look at the cord—try not to think about how he said he would tie me up. Not because it scares me but because it excites me.

He takes a sip, then offers the glass to me. I drink, too, the act of sharing the wine wonderfully intimate.

I draw a breath, and my eyes slide toward the cord. Despite everything I've done—and I've done a lot—I've never actually had a guy tie me down before. Nikki would say it's because I'm usually the one going after them—getting my kicks and blowing off steam—and that means that I need to be in control. Honestly, she'd probably be right.

With Ryan, though … well, with Ryan, I like the idea of him taking charge. I like it a lot.

I lick my lips, and hope I don't look too eager. "So," I say.

His smile is slow and lazy and wonderfully sexy. "So," he repeats.

"Are you going to tie me to the bed now?"

"Not exactly," he says with a kind of sensual mischief that creates a tug deep down in my belly. He nods to the bed. "Kneel for me."

I glance at the rope, then at the bed. Then I do as he asks. "Is this—I mean, are you—"

"Am I into BDSM? Am I a master? Do I want you to be my sub?"

I blink. *Well. Now that he put it that way…* "Um, yeah. I mean, are you? Do you?"

His smile is a little bit amused, a little bit smug. "I like being in control, kitten. I like giving pleasure, and I like receiving it. I like taking a woman as far as she can go. As far as I'm concerned, anything goes between two consenting adults. I don't give a fuck about labels. But yes, Jamie, I want to tie you up. I want to see you bound. I want to make you mine. So tell me now—do you want that, too?"

My mouth is dry, but somehow I manage to give the only possible answer. "Yes."

I think I see the flicker of relief in his eyes, and for some reason that small reaction calms my nerves. He wants me—wants this—as much as I do, and I realize with sudden understanding that whatever I give up is like a reciprocal gift to him.

He steps toward me, the cord in his hands. "Do you know what makes bondage so pleasurable?"

"The submission," I say, now putting my thoughts into words. "Losing yourself to the will of another. Giving in to his touch completely. Trusting him completely." I tilt my head to face him more directly. "And for you, it's knowing that a woman is at your mercy. That you're responsible for pleasure. For pain. That you can tease her and torment her." I draw in a shaky breath. "Don't torment me, Hunter. I want you too badly."

"And I, you," he says, then presses his lips to mine and kisses me tenderly.

He moves behind me and binds my ankles together as I kneel, then tells me to twine my hands together behind my back, but also under my rear, so it is almost as if I am sitting on my hands. He binds my wrists, and then uses a length of cord to connect my bound ankles to my bound wrists.

Not that I can see any of that, but I can feel most of what he is doing, and he tells me the rest. What I don't know is what he has in store for me now that I am trussed up like this. But when he moves back in front of me I tell him what I want. "You," I say. "I want you in my mouth."

In this position, I am mostly bent over, and he is kneeling in front of me. He is erect and huge, and I think greedily that I can take all of him. That I need all of him.

"Is that what you want?" he asks. "Why?"

"Maybe I want to take you to the edge," I say as desire presses down upon me.

"You want me at your mercy?" I can hear the smile in his voice.

"Yes," I say. "I do."

"Who am I to argue with a determined woman?"

He is already kneeling in front of me, and now he takes me by the hair. My position is unsteady, but I ease forward, teasing the tip of his cock with my tongue, then growing bolder when he groans, calling my name.

I draw him in, sucking and licking, tasting and teasing, and I know by the way he holds my head, by the way his hips thrust as he fucks my mouth, that this was the right thing. He has taken me to the edge over and over, but now I am taking him.

I suck and tease and use my tongue to play with the tip of him. He thrusts deep, but I've never had a problem giving head, and I take him in, all of him, wishing I could use my hands, too. I want to touch him, want to see him. I want to know that I am giving back to him some of the pleasure that he has given me.

And then, with a deep groan and a low cry of, "no, not yet," he pulls out. I hear his shallow breathing, and when I tilt my head up to see his face, it is passion I see in his eyes.

I lick my lips, savoring the taste of him as he repeats, "Not yet," more calmly this time. "I'm going to come inside you," he says, and my body clenches tight with his words. "I'm going to make you explode." He strokes my hair as he says, "I'm clean, but I'll wear a condom if you want."

I shake my head. "No. Please. I want to feel you."

He smiles in answer before he moves behind me, his hands stroking my rear as he trails kisses down my back. "Put your head down," he says. "I want to see your ass in the air."

I comply, and he strokes me, his hands sliding over the globes of my ass. "Do you have toys?" he asks.

"Not a lot," I say. "Some oil that I bought when we got Nikki her goody bag."

"Where?"

I point him to the bedside table, and he gets the stuff. The oil is some sort of minty arousal oil, and he strokes it onto my clit, then laughs softly when I first complain that I feel nothing—but then soon buck from the tingly, intense sensations. I'm desperately wet, and with his finger teasing my clit, I'm going a little crazy.

"I'm going to fuck you now," he says, then thrusts inside me. He's deep, and I moan in pleasure as he fills me. I rock back, wanting to take more of him, and as I do he pulls me to him, his free hand gripping my waist. Then he slides that hand down, teasing me where our bodies are joined, making his fingers slick before he slides them up to my ass. "I want you here, too," he says. "Have you ever?"

I shake my head. "Just toys," I say, as the sensation of the oil on my clit and his hand on my ass drives me very close to the edge. I feel a blush coming on. "I liked it."

"I'll remember that," he says. "Right now—right now I think I'm too far gone. Jesus, Jamie, what you do to me."

He thrusts again, deeper and faster, even as he teases and torments my clit, the effect of the oil shooting me up into the stratosphere. I hold my breath, willing the climax to wash over me, craving the explosion, desperate for the man to fill me.

And then, with one final thrust, he cries my name and empties himself into me. His hand presses against my clit, and the renewed pressure sends me tumbling over after him, faster and faster until there is nowhere to go, and he topples us both over onto the bed.

I am still bound, a tight ball, and he is curved around me. I am breathing deep, my mind little more than mush and my body like liquid. "Christ, Hunter. You destroyed me."

"No," he says. "It's you who've broken me. There's a fire in you, kitten. And I want to burn with you."

"Kitten," I repeat, my voice dreamy. "Why kitten?"

He chuckles. "I think it suits you." He kisses my shoulder. "You're soft and warm and definitely playful. But I'll need to watch the claws."

I have to bite back a laugh. "Yes," I say. "You will."

We lay that way for a moment, then he unties my bindings. I stretch, relishing the motion, as he reaches for the remote on the bedside table and presses the button to close the electronic blinds.

Then he pulls the quilt up over both of us and holds me close.

I spoon against him, his chest warm against my back, and his cock still semi-hard against my rear. He drapes his arm around me and holds me close.

I could get used to this, I think.

Hell, I could get used to him.

Except for the short nap by the pool, I haven't slept in almost two days and exhaustion presses down on me. I close my eyes, feeling warm and satisfied and sweetly used, and, finally, let sleep sweep me away.

Chapter Five

When my eyes flutter open, I do not know how much time has passed. Very little, I think, as we are still in the same position. But the gentle softness that drew me into sleep is gone, replaced by something cold and panicky.

I do not remember my dreams, but I am damn certain that my subconscious has been poking her manicured fingernail hard into my ass.

I don't want to wake him, and so I gently lift his arm, then slide out from under it. He doesn't move, and I take a moment to sit on the edge of the bed and look at him. Even in sleep there's a strength to him, and he really is so damn good-looking that I could just sit here all day drinking him in.

He makes me feel amazing—sensual, sexual, special. But it's not just sex. There's something about Ryan Hunter—about the way we connect—that makes me smile. We click. We always have, even without the touching, the fucking.

I like him, I think.

More than that, I could love him.

The thought churns up that undercurrent of panic, making it rise to the top. Turning my skin cold and prickly.

The last time I fell for a guy, I got my heart ripped out and stomped upon. Bryan Raine, a narcissistic asshole who was a major catalyst for The Plan. A man who pulled me in and twisted me up.

Granted, Bryan Raine isn't even worthy to lick Ryan's boots, but when you get down to it, my panic isn't about Ryan. It's about me.

And I fucked up.

No matter how amazing these last few hours were—no matter how wonderful he made me feel—I blew it big-time. Like I had with Raine. Like I had with so many guys.

I mean, for fuck's sake, all I asked of myself was that I go home and get my shit together. And then one hot guy tells me he wants me in his bed, and I start panting like a bitch in heat.

Pathetic.

Frustrated and angry with myself, I stand up. My phone is on the bedside table, and I can see on the lock screen that I've missed a call. I take it with me to the bathroom, and as I'm in there I listen to the voice message. It's from Georgia Myers, the head of programming for the network television affiliate I'd auditioned for in Dallas.

I listen, my heart pounding faster and faster, as she offers me the job.

"I understand you're currently out of town, but I'm still hoping that you can start right away. This is a little unorthodox, but our public relations director used to work in Los Angeles, and she has some contacts in the film industry. You may be aware that the new Derrick Johnson movie is filming in Las Vegas," she adds, referring to the hottest new director in town. "We've actually been granted access to some of the cast. It's a pretty big coup for a local affiliate station, and we're very excited by the opportunity."

She continues, asking me to call and let her know if I can take the job and, if so, if I can get to Vegas quickly. She'll find out who among the cast is available for an interview and e-mail me the research material.

That pounding in my chest increases as my panic takes on a new quality. A this-is-a-fucking-awesome-opportunity I-don't-want-to-screw-it-up quality.

I won't, I think. *I can't.*

I can do this job. I look good on camera. I'm comfortable talking with people. This is the kind of job I want. The kind of job I need.

It's the kind of job in which I can prove myself—and the kind of job that can lead me right back to Los Angeles when I'm clear.

In other words, it's step one of The Plan already checked off the list.

I start to race out of the bathroom, eager to tell Ryan—and then I pull myself up short in the doorway. What the hell am I doing?

I could get used to this, I'd thought as I slid out of bed earlier.

And damn me all to hell, it was true. I *could* get used to it. Already he's filled my head and knocked me off center. Already, he is the first person I wanted to share good news with.

Oh, god. Oh, god. I really have fucked up and good. I should have walked away. Should have told him no.

But I'm a goddamn wimp who can't even stick to her own decisions. Who gets so twisted up by a man she can't even manage to follow her own path.

Worse than that, I let him take control. I let him get close. I dropped my shields and surrendered totally.

I've given him the power to hurt me—and I know goddamn well that eventually he will do just that.

They always do.

How had I screwed it up so badly? I'd gone from being determined to stand strong and get my shit together to drowning in the residue of all my bad choices.

I look at the man sleeping soundly in the bed. I know what will happen when he wakes. He will soothe my tears, tell me it will be okay. He'll heal my wounds with kisses, and before I know it, I'll be on my back with his cock inside me, my job and my plan all but forgotten.

I tell myself I am strong enough to resist. That I will tell him and then simply walk away.

But I know better. I want him—his touch, his kisses. If he wakes, I will stay.

And I will hate myself—and him—for it.

I turn, lost, and stumble back to the bathroom counter. I blink back tears and stare at my reflection. "Do something," I say to the girl who looks back at me. "Fix this."

And so I do the only thing I can think to do—I run.

Chapter Six

I'm sorry.

That's all I wrote on the note that I left on the bedside table. I wanted to say more, but I'm not good at saying the words, and I'm even worse at psychoanalyzing myself.

And I'm certain that *I had to go—I have to get my shit together, and you scare the crap out of me* wouldn't have been the best approach, even if it was true.

I've been driving for two hours now, and the sun has long since disappeared behind the San Bernardino mountains that fill my rearview mirror.

I'd made my escape quietly, wearing only the jeans and T-shirt that I'd left in the bathroom, and taking only my purse and phone. I'd brought a suitcase with me to California, of course, and my suite was littered with shopping bags. But I hadn't bothered with any of that because there was no way for me to pack and not wake up Ryan.

So I'd run, knowing full well that I could call Gregory, Damien's valet, in the morning and have him gather my things and ship them to my parents in Texas.

As for the Vegas job—well, I had makeup in my purse, but I guess I'd just have to suck it up and shop for clothes. I figured that counted as retail therapy, and even considering the damage that I would undoubtedly do to my credit card, it would be cheaper than a round of sessions with a shrink.

I'd taken the Ferrari from where Damien had left it for me in his impressive underground garage. It had taken concentration to get out of Malibu because I tend to get turned around on all the twisting roads, but as soon as I hit the highway, I started thinking about Ryan. About leaving.

About the way he made me feel.

Twice, I reached for my phone, then yanked my hand back before I could close my fingers tight around it. When I reached for it a third time, I snatched it up, then powered the damn thing off and tossed it in the glove box.

Out of sight, out of mind. Except while that worked to stifle the urge to call him, it did nothing to stifle the thoughts and memories and emotions that rattled in my head. The memory of his mouth upon me, his cock inside me. The image of his face as he gazed at me with such tenderness. My own admonitions telling me to run—to get clear. Ryan's stern pronouncement that he liked me wild—but that he wouldn't let me walk.

But I did walk—hell, I did more than walk. I ran.

And now, on the road, I am second-guessing myself all over again.

Fuck it.

I've been listening to my own thoughts for two hours and I can't stand it anymore. I check the mirrors to confirm that I'm the only car on this stretch of Interstate 15, then snatch my phone out of the glove box and power it back on.

I fiddle with the radio until I finally figure out how to set it for auxiliary and turn on Bluetooth. A few more adjustments, and I'm jamming to one of the many playlists I keep on my phone. A mix of classic and new rock, along with a few heavy metal songs to add a little pop to the mix. It's loud enough and rough enough to keep me from thinking—and that is exactly what I want.

Considering how densely populated Los Angeles is, this stretch of California is like culture shock. I passed Barstow at least thirty minutes ago, and since then I've seen only one other car on the road. More recently, a sign announced the town of Yermo, but it must have been off the highway because as I cruised by in the dark, I'd seen nothing but the long, narrow tunnel of my own headlights.

Honestly, it's a little freaky.

I've made the drive from Los Angeles to Vegas a number of times, so I know more or less where I am and that I have about two hours of absolute nothingness ahead of me until I see the brilliance of Vegas filling up the night sky. That means I'll be rolling into town just after midnight, which is fine by me. The city will still be hopping. I can grab some breakfast at a diner, and then I can go crash.

Sex—and my nap—had reinvigorated me some, but I am starting to fade again. It's hard not to when I am blanketed in black, lost in the seemingly endless abyss of the Mojave Desert at night.

The car shudders slightly, and I frown, wondering if I've just run over some debris. When it does it again, I click off the music so that I can actually think. I check the rearview mirror, but I can see nothing there in the pitch black.

I take my hands off the steering wheel, but the Ferrari continues straight, so I rule out a flat tire. It shudders again and then slows. I press harder on the accelerator, but that does nothing. Automatically, my eyes go to the gas gauge, but I still have almost half a tank, so that isn't the problem. Maybe it's something electrical? Or maybe—

Shit.

Damien had warned me about the broken gas gauge at least a million times, and Nikki had reminded me again earlier today. And still all it took was a gorgeous man to completely empty my head of any and all useful facts.

And now I'm going to have to wait for AAA, which, of course, will take forever.

I steer onto the shoulder, but keep my foot on the accelerator, living the absurd fantasy that maybe I'll reach a convenience store, gas station, five-star hotel. *Something.*

But when the Ferrari gives its last gasp of life, I look out as far as the headlights reach and see absolutely nothing. I look left and right, hoping to see the flicker of light from a house or from a business.

Nothing.

Neither are there lights approaching in my rearview mirror or coming toward me, westbound toward the coast.

Shit.

Apparently, I'm stuck. Isn't that just peachy?

I put the car in park, kill the engine, and turn on the hazard lights. Then I snatch up my phone and search my contacts for the

800 number for AAA, but when I dial, the call immediately fails. I spit out a curse, then try again, and only when the call fails once more do I think to glance at my phone's signal strength.

No service.

What the fuck? How can there be no service? This is America for fuck's sake, where everyone and their dog has a cell phone and wants to be able to use it. And, seriously, isn't one of the primary reasons for owning a cell phone so that you can make a call when you're in trouble? And yet the Powers That Be don't put cell towers in scary, empty parts of the country where stranded women may need to make a phone call so that they don't have to wait in a Ferrari for the next car—which just might be driven by a sex-crazed psychopath?

I exhale, pissed, and beat my palm against the steering wheel. Then I open my door, thinking that I'll just start walking.

Then I immediately close my door and lock it because the walking plan is just about as stupid as it gets, especially now that I have sex-crazed psychopaths on the brain.

Okay. Fine. This is not a problem.

Well, yes it is. But it's not an insurmountable problem.

I pull my phone out again and stare at the screen as if that will magically make a signal appear.

Since I do not actually have magical abilities, nothing happens. But I open my text messaging program anyway. I read somewhere that text messages don't require as strong a signal, and also that the strength of a cell tower's signal changes all the time. So maybe if I send a text, eventually it will find a signal and flitter away to its destination.

Clearly, there is a reason that I am an actress and not an

engineer. But I figure that even if it doesn't help, it won't hurt.

I open the messaging app and stare at the phone. Because the first person I think of to text is Ryan—and yet how the hell am I supposed to phrase it? *Sorry I skipped out on you. Please come save me.*

Somehow, that doesn't work for me.

I consider texting Sylvia, Damien's secretary with whom Nikki and I have become friends, but I'm certain that she will simply send Ryan. He is, after all, Stark International's security dude. Evelyn Dodge, my friend and pseudo-agent, would be a great choice, but I happen to know that she and her lover Blaine left around lunchtime for a Manhattan getaway.

I tell myself I'm being stupid. That Ryan will be mad, yes, but he won't leave me stranded. I'm his boss's new wife's best friend, after all. So even if he doesn't come himself, he'll send someone else.

Besides, odds are the text will never go through.

I spend a few moments thinking about it, then decide on the message.

Sorry I bolted, but I need help. Stranded on the 15 just past Yermo. Please?

I read it once more, then press "send" before I can talk myself out of it. Then I put in my headphones, turn my music back on, lean back in my seat, and wait.

If nothing else, I figure I'll be rescued come morning. There will be more traffic, for one thing, and maybe even the highway patrol.

As it turns out, I don't have to wait that long.

Not even five minutes have passed when I see the flash of lights in the rearview mirror. I turn off the music and watch the car approach. I can't tell what kind it is; all I can see is the glare of the lights as it crawls closer and closer, moving at a snail's pace now.

It is still on the highway, but as I watch it slides to the right, pulling off onto the shoulder. Then it eases forward until it is right behind me.

I expect the driver to kill the lights, but he or she doesn't, and I am left sitting there in my Please Carjack Me Now Ferrari with sex fiends on my mind.

My pulse starts to beat more quickly, and I curse myself for not getting the tire iron out of the trunk. Because there's not a damn thing I can use as a weapon inside the vehicle—not unless I intend to beat someone senseless with my iPhone.

I am astounded at my naiveté and pissed off at my own stupidity. I passed through Barstow with its stretch of gas stations and I was so busy trying not to think that I didn't think. And now here I am, trapped in a car with Ted Bundy parked behind me.

I check the phone once more, but it still shows no signal.

Fuck.

I see the door to the car open, and someone gets out. A man, I think, though I can see very little in the dark in my mirror.

I check the door locks again and am relieved to find them secure.

He is approaching the car now, walking with the light at his back so that he appears as only the shadow of a man. I tell myself to be calm, that he is probably just a Good Samaritan. That most serial killers are not trolling the interstates.

I know it. I believe it, and I'm still scared shitless. Terrified that Ryan will get my text and two hours later will arrive at the

Ferrari to find me battered and bloodied and very much dead.

Stop it. Just stop it, already.

And then he's there—his torso right by my window—and his firm rap on the door combines with my nerves to rip a scream from my throat.

The man bends down, and I suck in a gasp that is part surprise, part fear, part wonder.

Because I'm staring at a man who can't possibly be there.

I'm staring at Ryan Hunter.

Chapter Seven

I fly out of the car, then pound my fists on his chest. "Dammit, Ryan! Goddammit, you scared me to death!"

He pulls me close and strokes my back, waiting for me to calm down. I breathe him in, letting his familiar scent soothe me, letting his strength calm me. "It's okay, kitten. You're fine. Come on, Jamie. You're safe."

I hold tight, breathing deep until the terror has passed and I feel calm again.

Calm and mortified.

I ease out of his arms, taking a step backward. The night is so thick that I can see his face only in the thin light from the Ferrari's interior that spills out from the still-open door. I see the concern. The hint of worry that is fading in his eyes now that I am steady again.

I don't want to see the anger that I know is coming, and yet I can't stand here and pretend to still be scared just so that I can put off the inevitable.

I draw in a breath, tilt my head back so that I can see him, and whisper, "I'm sorry."

I expect anger. I expect fury. But the soul-deep sadness that fills his eyes is more than I can handle.

"Hunter," I say, my voice choked. "Please, just let me—"

He nods at the car parked behind the Ferrari. "Get in," he says in a voice that broaches no argument.

"But—" I lick my lips. "I can't go back. I have to get to Vegas."

"I'll take you where you need to go, Jamie," he says, and now I hear the anger bubbling up from somewhere dark and deep. "Now get in the goddamn car."

Since he is more than capable of simply picking me up and tossing me inside—and since at the moment he looks prepared to do just that—I do as he says.

It's a Mercedes, smooth and sleek with a leather interior and that incredible new-car smell. I put the seat belt on, kick off my shoes, and draw my knees to my chest.

I watch as he leans into the Ferrari, then emerges with the keys and my phone. He comes to the Mercedes, opens the door, and gets in without saying a word.

For a moment, he just sits there, and I think that he is finally going to speak. Then he presses the button to start the car, puts it in gear, and pulls onto the highway. In seconds, the Ferrari is behind us, and I twist in my seat to watch it disappear in the distance.

"We can't just leave it."

He looks at me, and I swear if he stays silent I'm going to scream. Thankfully, he answers. "I'll take care of it." His words are clipped. Measured. "I'll have someone get her to Vegas."

"Good," I say. "Perfect."

He looks at me curiously, but doesn't ask why I'm determined to reach Vegas before Texas, and so I decide not to tell. Instead, I ask what is on my mind. "How did you find me?"

"I'm the head of security for Stark International. Do you really think I'd allow Damien to drive a car that doesn't have a tracking device installed?"

"Oh." I frown. That hadn't occurred to me. And I suppose if it had, I would have assumed the device had been removed once Damien gave the car to me. "Okay, then." I lick my lips. "In that case, *why* did you follow me?"

The muscle in his jaw tightens, and I brace myself for the explosion. But when he speaks, his voice is surprisingly soft. "You left in a hurry, without any of your things. I was worried," he says, taking his eyes off the road to look at me. "Turns out I had reason to be."

I nod. "Thank you," I say. And then I add, "I really am sorry."

He doesn't answer, and a thick, uncomfortable silence fills the car.

I want to reach for him, to put my hand on his.

I want to give him comfort, but I know that is something I am no longer entitled to do. So instead I lean my head back and close my eyes, giving in to the sudden, cloying exhaustion that has settled upon me.

I don't plan to sleep, but I must have dozed off because I am jerked awake when the car slows and the texture of the pavement beneath the tires changes.

I blink out the window and see a small, squat building in front of us.

"Where are we?" I ask sleepily.

"Baker," he says. "We're staying here until morning."

"What? But I need to get to Vegas."

"Not past midnight you don't. And I'd rather you get there alive." He pulls into a parking space and kills the engine. Then he turns to face me. "I'm tired, Jamie. I was up all night before the wedding, and then throughout the party. I didn't get much sleep after that, either," he adds.

He looks at me, his expression cool. "I'm running on fumes, and I know you are, too. So we are staying here, and we are going to sleep."

"Fine," I say because what else is there to say?

As far as I can tell, this is the only motel in Baker, and it's tiny. It's also almost completely sold out, which I find surprising. There is only one room, and it has a king-size bed. When Ryan tells me this, I stoically nod my head. Secretly, though, I am worried. I ran because I believed it was the right choice—and because I am weak.

I am still weak, and simply having him nearby makes me weaker. I cannot remember ever being as affected by a man as I am by Ryan Hunter. And if he makes a move during the night, I'm not at all certain I will have the strength to say no.

Because the truth is, though I am certain that going back to Texas is the right thing, I regret the way I ran from him. I regret even more the nights I lost with him.

Maybe The Plan really is only about Texas. And maybe taking the memory of Ryan Hunter back with me would have made me stronger.

And maybe I'm pulling rationalizations out of my ass to justify sleeping with him in this tiny hotel.

Right. Best to just not go there.

The room is small and dingy and smells like old socks. There is a lumpy bed and a threadbare armchair.

I sit in the armchair.

Ryan doesn't sit at all. Instead he paces, and I know him well enough to see that he is debating something. I presume it's whether or not to yell at me.

I decide to dive in. I figure I owe him that much. "I'm sorry," I say for about the four millionth time.

He sighs, then sits on the edge of the bed facing me. "Just tell me why. Because honestly, Jamie, I'm baffled. I thought we were having a good time. I know damn well that I was."

"Me, too," I say, my voice small but earnest.

"And I thought we'd reached an understanding. I thought I'd made it perfectly clear that I wasn't going to be one of the men you tossed away. And I sure as hell thought that we were on the same page about you not simply sneaking away."

"I fucked up," I say. My breath shudders and I feel tears sting my eyes. "I didn't want to hurt you. Or piss you off."

"You managed both," he says, and when I look at his face, I see something vulnerable in his eyes.

I open my mouth to say that I'm sorry again, but then I stay silent. I have said those empty words too many times already.

"Dammit, Jamie." He sounds ripped up, and I force myself not to reach for him when he kneels down in front of me, his hands on my knees. "I want you, make no mistake. But if I can't have you in my bed, I still want you in my life."

My heart stutters. He's speaking words of friendship, not just sex. Of a connection that's more than just physical. It scares me— but even as I want to shrink away, I also can't deny the little spark of hope that is now dancing inside me.

He reaches up and strokes my cheek. "I care about you," he says. "And I thought—"

"What?" I'm breathless.

"I thought you felt the same."

"I do. It's just—" I stand up and run my fingers through my hair, trying to find the words. "You've seen me. And I know you've heard stories. It's not like I keep my private life a secret, and that whole fiasco with Bryan Raine was all over the tabloids."

Raine is an up-and-coming movie star, and it hadn't ended well. Primarily because he was a selfish, self-absorbed prick who decided to dump me because it would be better for his career to screw an actress with clout.

"I fuck around," I say, which pretty much sums up my entire adult life. "And it's messed me up a lot. Bryan messed with my head. And then I went and slept with one of my best friends, and we managed to fuck that relationship up, too."

I'm rattling my thoughts out, not sure if I'm revealing too much or too little, if I'm pushing him away or driving him closer.

"But then with you," I continue. "I've never felt so—" I shake my head because I'm not going there. "It was amazing," I say, backtracking. "But the timing was completely messed up. I was already supposed to go back. I was already deep into The Plan."

"The Plan?"

"The whole reason I moved back to Texas in the first place. I need to get my head on straight. I've done a hell of a lot of dumb stuff."

"Everyone's done dumb stuff, kitten," he says. "Running isn't going to make you smarter. It just puts more distance between you and the problem."

I shake my head. "It's not about distance. It's not even about avoiding sex. Not really. But sex knocks me off track, and I need to stay strong."

"All right," he says. "But if it's not about distance and not about sex, then what is it about?"

That's a good question, and not one I was sure I had the answer to. "It's about...I guess it's about figuring out who you are. Who I am. Does that sound foolish?"

He shakes his head, then moves to sit back on the bed opposite my chair. "No," he says. "It doesn't. Do you think you're going to figure it out in Texas?"

"Yeah," I say. "By way of Vegas," I add, and then tell him about the job.

"It sounds like an excellent opportunity," he says.

"It is. And I think I'll be good at it."

"I know you will." He stands up, paces the room, then stops in front of me. "All right," he says.

I'm confused. "All right?"

"I'm not going to argue with you, and I'm certainly not going to force you. If you think you need to make a quest and go home, then I won't stop you."

His expression is warm but intense. "I already know who you are, Jamie Archer. But I also know you have to figure it out on your own."

His phone chimes, and he pulls it from his pocket, then glances at me, amused. "You texted me to rescue you?"

"I—oh. Yeah. Sorry. I realize it's a little weird seeing as how I walked out on you, but..." I trail off in a shrug. "You were the first one I thought to text, so I tried to think of other people. But I couldn't, and so...at any rate, it doesn't matter. You rescued me even before I asked."

He moves back in front of me, then reaches down and pulls me to my feet. "Thank you," he says simply.

I shake my head in confusion. "For what?"

"For knowing that I will always be there for you, no matter what."

"Ryan..." My voice is soft and full of emotion. Because he is right. I do know that, and the knowledge wraps around me like a soft blanket.

He smiles in what I think is understanding. Then the smile intensifies, and a hint of amusement touches his lips. "If getting to Texas is what you need, then I'll get you there. First Vegas, then on to Dallas."

"I can drive myself," I say.

"Maybe," he says. "But do you really want to? I provide a quality transportation service," he adds with a cocky grin. "And all for a very reasonable price."

"Price," I repeat, amused. "What kind of price?"

"I'll make you a deal," he says. "And since we're going to Vegas, we'll let roulette decide the terms."

"I'm still not following you," I say.

"Then let me be more clear. One spin of the roulette wheel. Black, you pay me. Red, you fuck me."

I gape at him. "But I just told you. Getting my head straight. Sex. How it messes me up, and—"

"You said it wasn't about avoiding sex. Just that sex knocks you off track. But I'll be keeping you on track, Jamie. First Vegas, then Dallas, and then I go back to LA, no questions asked."

"I—"

"We won't be dating," he says. "Nothing like that. Just the same terms as before." The heat in his voice is unmistakable. "You. At my mercy."

I swallow. My head says I should say no, but every other part of my body is screaming for me to say yes.

I lick my lips. "And the payment? If it's black, I mean?"

"I'm salaried at Stark International. But I'll calculate my hourly rate. We can start the clock when we arrive in Vegas."

I narrow my eyes. "How much exactly," I demand. He does a quick calculation and tells me a number that comes near to making me faint.

"Are you insane? I can't afford that."

"Well then," he says with a wicked grin, "you'd better hope for red."

Chapter Eight

Because we slept until almost noon and then had an absolutely fabulous breakfast of greasy eggs, bacon, and melt-in-your-mouth biscuits at the motel's dive of a coffee shop, it is already past four when we finally roll into Vegas.

Even in the daylight, the city feels alive.

If Manhattan is your snooty stepmother and Los Angeles your hippie brother, then Las Vegas is your crazy-ass cousin who doesn't know what to be when he grows up.

Everything is gaudy, bright, and larger than life. Paris bumps up against Egypt, and the whole place has a Disneyland feel to it.

It's probably terribly wrong of me to love it, but I do. Especially the Strip, where all the biggest and best casinos and hotels line up like a receiving line, welcoming everyone, from people with Stark-like billions all the way down to me, with my nearly empty checking account.

I gawk out the window as we drive, feeling a bit like an eager puppy taking in the sights. I don't even gamble much, and I still love Vegas. I think I feel a camaraderie with it. We're both a little bit tacky sometimes.

We pass the iconic Caesar's Palace, and moments later, pull up in front of the magnificent Starfire Resort. The drive circles a fountain, and I watch, mesmerized as colorful columns of water rise and fall.

A bellman hurries to open my door while a valet takes the car from Ryan.

"Shall we?" Ryan asks, taking my arm.

"I've never stayed here before," I say. "I'm pretty much a low-rent end of the Strip kind of girl."

"You'll love it. And I'm not surprised the producers are putting the actors up here. Starfire is one of the most luxurious hotels on the Strip."

I'd received the follow-up e-mail from Georgia while we were on the road. The station has booked me a room at the Starfire, and I have an interview scheduled the next morning with Ellison Ward, a British actor who is all the rage now that he's won an Oscar. They've even flown in a cameraman to do the filming. All I need to do is review the file, tweak the suggested questions, and not screw up.

When I first read the e-mail, I was surprised that a Dallas station could arrange a one-on-one with somebody of Ward's stature. But after I read the research material, I understood. Apparently Ward's mother lived in Texas for a few years and had a fondness for The Metroplex that she'd passed on to her son.

Honestly, it was quite a coup for the station and for me. Undoubtedly, the piece would go national, and I'd get some serious exposure, all of which would help in my quest to get back to LA someday.

That, of course, only made the "don't screw up" part of the equation all the more important.

An efficient young woman in a pencil-style skirt and tailored blouse meets us as we step into the stunning lobby decorated in what I think is an Art Deco style. "Mr. Hunter, Ms. Archer. We have you all set. Would you like to follow me?"

"That's okay," Ryan says. "We need to go to the casino first. The room is ready?"

The girl nods. "Absolutely. Enjoy your stay, and don't hesitate to ring if you need anything."

I glance at Ryan, slightly confused. "Efficient staff."

"Very," he says as she moves across the tiled floor to the registration desk.

"Time for roulette?" I ask, the word alone sending a few tingles running through me.

He trails his fingers down my arm. "Roulette," he confirms.

The casino opens off the lobby, and we can hear the noise and bluster as we head down the set of staircases to the wide, slot-machine lined entrance. It's like entering a different world. Noise and lights. The chatter of patrons, the calls of the staff. And beneath it all, the clink and clank of coins.

"This way," he says, leading me down a tiled path that is cut through the carpeted areas that hold the banks of slot machines, tables for blackjack and other card games, craps, and the like. We find the roulette tables on the far side, and by the time we arrive, I feel as though I have walked a thousand miles.

"Pick your table," he says, and since they all seem the same to me, I choose the closest one. He pulls a fifty dollar casino chip out of his jacket pocket, which strikes me as a bit odd since I never saw him exchange any money for chips. I don't have time to think about it, though, because he places the chip in my hand and tells me to bet.

Immediately, I put the chip on red.

Ryan laughs, then lifts my hand and kisses my fingertips, the touch as gentle as a butterfly's wing and at least as sensual.

"What's so funny?" I ask.

"You're giving away your secrets, kitten," he says, nodding to the table where I'd placed my bet. "You know what red means."

"I do," I say, and then, because I'm feeling bold and I really do want it, I move to his side and lift myself up on my toes so that I can whisper in his ear. "It means that I'm at your mercy," I say, and then slowly—very slowly—I run my tongue over the curve of his ear.

I'm holding on to him as I do it, one hand on his shoulder, the other on his back. I feel the way his body tightens beneath my touch. I hear the low groan that he tries to stifle, and, yes, I smile.

"Naughty," he whispers as I lower myself. But I just gaze innocently at the table and the wheel that has started to spin.

I hold my breath as the ball bounces, around and around, and then—*yes*—it lands on red. I glance sideways and see that Ryan is watching me. I smile triumphantly. "I had to want red," I tease. "There was no way I could come up with enough cash to pay you."

He laughs. "Fair enough, kitten. I promise, though, that I'll make sure that landing on red was very much worth it. For both of us." He nods at the table as the croupier pays out our winnings. "Care to stay in the casino and gamble a bit longer? I'm feeling lucky."

"I'm feeling lucky, too," I say. "And I absolutely do not want to stay."

He makes a noise I interpret as satisfaction, then pockets our winnings. He takes my arm and leads me out of the casino. I'm completely turned around, but I'm pretty sure we've been moving away from the lobby. My instinct is confirmed when I realize that we are in a wide-open, bright shopping area. The ceiling is a mural of the sky, arching across the space above our heads from sunrise on one side to sunset on the other, with day and night between.

In the area in which we are standing, the night sky is spread above us, and thousands of small electric lights wink down at us. It's cheesy, but it's also romantic, and when Ryan takes my hand to lead me through the mall, I cannot stifle my little sigh of contentment.

For right now, anyway, all is well in my world.

Like most of the shops on the pricier section of the Strip, the ones that fill this mall are high-end, full of designer goods and hefty price tags. Those extravagant items are balanced with markdowns so that the overall result is a store full of products for both the lucky and not-so-lucky gambler.

We pass by a window display overflowing with diamonds and emeralds, along with price tags that make clear that this is not the store for part-time gamblers and two-bit winners. This is where the high rollers come to shop.

Ryan takes my hand and leads me inside.

"That would look lovely on your wrist," he says, pointing to a diamond and platinum bracelet that costs more than my condo.

"You're insane," I say.

He grins at me. "Not your style?"

"No," I admit because my taste tends toward funkier.

He eyes me critically, his gaze skimming up and down. "No," he murmurs, "you're right. You need something more..." His voice drifts off as he walks the length of the glass counter. A clerk comes by, apparently sniffing a sale, but Ryan waves him away with a flick of his hand. "Like this," he says, pointing to a circle of lovely pounded silver. It is a choker-style necklace made so that it catches the light at a variety of angles. There is a hinge on the back with a pin that fits through a corresponding cylinder to keep the thing in place. At the center there is a single loop upon which one could hang a charm.

"It's lovely," I say.

"It's practical," he says.

I raise a brow in question.

"The loop," he says. "So simple to attach a leash."

Oh. I swallow. "It's like a slave collar," I say, then lick my lips. "Is that why you think it suits me?" I say in a voice full of challenge. "Because right now, I belong to you?"

He looks straight at me. "Yes." The word is simple and direct and so full of meaning it makes me tremble. I think of the way he bound me back in Malibu. The pleasure of surrendering to his mercy.

I remember, and it makes me wet.

I turn, then leave the store, going back out into the mall, my breath now shallow.

He follows me, and when I look up to meet his eyes, I find I cannot read his expression.

"Did you leave because the idea makes you uncomfortable?"

I consider lying. It would be so easy to just say the words and walk away.

But I don't want to. I want the truth between us. I want to see where we go. "No," I say. "I left because I like it."

His expression doesn't change. Only the slight increase in the tension of his jaw lets me know that my answer has gotten to him. "All right," he says, and then continues to walk down the wide, store-lined corridor.

I follow, a little on edge. I'm not sure he understands my confession. Or, if he does, what that means for me.

As far as I can tell, though, the subject is dropped.

"So what are we shopping for?" I ask after five minutes have passed in silence.

"You, of course." He gestures to the jeans and T-shirt I've been wearing for two days now. "You can't live in those clothes."

The man has a point.

"At the very least, you'll need something for dinner tonight," he says. "And something for tomorrow's interview. Here," he says, pausing in front of a store wherein every item probably costs more than my entire credit card limit.

"I can't afford this," I whisper as we step through the door.

He shoots me an amused expression. "I can."

The store is apparently arranged by layer, and the first thing I see when we enter is a bin with lingerie. He reaches in and pulls out a pair of thong-style panties. He looks at them, then looks at me. I try to keep a straight face, but the whole idea of him picking out my panties is amusing me. "Why bother?" I finally say. "I'm just going to take them off."

"I certainly hope so," he replies with at least as much humor. "But that's part of the fun."

I swallow because he's definitely called that right.

He lifts a finger to signal a salesgirl, and she comes running. He hands her the panties, along with a few other pairs in assorted colors, then tells her we need a business outfit and an evening gown. She practically genuflects toward the both of us as she leads us further back to the uncluttered displays of designer clothing.

We handle the interview suit first, and as Ryan waits on a low, black leather couch, I go into the dressing room to change. I try on three options and end up going with a classic black suit and a white silk shell. It's more conservative than my usual style, but when we match it with three-inch black pumps, I can't deny that I look sexy as hell.

"You're going to knock 'em dead."

"Hopefully not Ellison Ward," I say. "It would be one hell of a story, but I'd rather have the interview in my portfolio."

He laughs and kisses me, then signals again for the salesgirl and tells her we're ready to see evening wear.

Though all the dresses she suggests are stunning, there is only one that I truly fall in love with. It is modeled after Marilyn Monroe's dress from *The Seven Year Itch*, the one with the full skirt that blows up when she stands over the subway grate. I love the way it drapes and the way the halter is both revealing and subtle. Most of all, I love the flirty, flippy skirt.

I hope it looks as good on me as it does on the hanger.

"Try it on," Ryan says, but this time he follows me to the dressing room. I see the clerk's eyes widen, but Ryan simply smiles. "I'll be joining the lady."

"Oh. Of course."

She backs away but not before giving Ryan a quick once-over. Then she glances at me. I have the distinct impression that right then, she would very much like to trade places with me.

I resist the urge to gloat and move into the dressing room, my skin tingly and my pulse pounding.

"What exactly are you doing?" I ask when he latches the door behind him.

"Watching you." He takes a seat on the upholstered ottoman that takes up one corner of the dressing room.

Since this is a high-end store, the dressing room is reasonably sized and the doors go all the way to the floor, providing genuine privacy. I face the three-way mirror and peel off my T-shirt and jeans, all the while watching Ryan's face in the reflection. He is making no effort to hide the heat, the desire, and I run my teeth over my lower lip, wishing that he would touch me.

He doesn't, though, and so I continue gamely on. Since the dress is backless, I unfasten my bra, then let it fall to the floor. I meet Ryan's eyes in the mirror, then draw my hands down over my breasts, my nipples as hard as beads, and then down to my tiny panties. I leave those on—though I'm tempted to strip fully.

But this isn't my show. The game is that I am at Ryan's mercy, not the other way around, and though I am frustrated that he has yet to touch me, I can't deny that I enjoy the tease—as well as this rising anticipation, so keen that it prickles my skin, making me aware of even the simple brush of air against me.

I take the dress off the hanger, then slip it on. It fits like a dream and feels like one against my skin. I stroke my hands over the soft material of the skirt, then give a little gasp of delight when I discover the hidden pocket.

I do a twirl for Ryan to show it off, then turn the pocket out. "I love this," I say. "The dress and the pocket. It's very retro. So a girl doesn't have to take her purse for an evening out. This is all you need for a credit card, a key, maybe even a small lipstick."

"I'll carry whatever you need tonight," he says. "And I'm less interested in pockets than in the way you look. And Jamie, you look amazing."

I turn back around to face my reflection, and I have to agree. My summer tan makes the white dress look even more vibrant, and there's something about the shape of it that flatters me, showing off all my curves to just the right effect.

Right now, my hair is in a very messy ponytail, but I can imagine it piled upon my head. I'll wear minimal makeup, just a light gloss of mascara and blood-red lipstick.

Yeah, I think, *I want this dress. I want to be on Ryan's arm in this dress.*

"I love it," I tell him.

He stands and moves behind me. I expect him to touch me, but he doesn't. But he is standing so close that I can feel his heat, his presence, and I pull it close around me, drawing in the thought of him. Feeling safe. And, yes, feeling loved.

When I meet his eyes in the mirror, my smile is tentative, even a little shy. And even so, the moment is perfect. "Thank you," I say.

"For the dress?"

"For everything."

Chapter Nine

Ryan carries the garment bag as we move across the Starfire lobby to the guest elevators.

"Remind me to get a picture of me in the dress," I say. "I want to e-mail it to my mom. She'd absolutely love it. Although Daddy would love it more. On her," I add, glancing sideways at him. "He loves to dress my mom up and take her out."

"How long have they been married?"

"Almost thirty years. I'm an only, which isn't surprising." I say the last without thinking and immediately regret it.

"Why's that?"

I shrug. I don't really want to get into it, and yet at the same time, I like talking to Ryan. He understands so much even without me speaking. And while I adore my parents, I also know that they're constantly under the surface in everything I do.

Nikki gets it, but compared to her life, mine is roses and candy.

I draw in a breath as we wait for the elevator, then lift a shoulder. "It sounds goofy, but they're so much in love that it scares me sometimes."

"I'm not following."

"I told you it sounded silly." I try to explain what it was like growing up with them. "I was like the third person on a hot date," I say. "They loved me, don't get me wrong, but we never felt like a family unit. There was always *them*. Or maybe *them plus me*. There was never *us*." I shrug again. "Like I said, it sounds stupid and petty."

"No," he says gently. "It doesn't. Your parents are your first conception of love, the first object of your love. You love them wholly and unconditionally, and expect that back. When you don't get that in return, it colors everything."

I gape at him, amazed that he understands so completely what it has taken me a lifetime to wrap my head around. And since he understands, I tell him the rest. "The thing is, my mom used to want to go to law school. And my dad loved to paint. But neither one does that anymore. My dad didn't want my mom to be away so much, so she never pursued her degree. And Mom doesn't give a crap about painting, so he stopped doing it. They're still deliriously happy together, but they've lost something. Part of themselves, I guess."

I don't say the next. I don't tell him that it terrifies me. That I'm afraid that's what happens when you find the one person that you love in all the world—they draw you into a bubble. A happy bubble, but one that is less vibrant and less colorful than the world you wanted to live in.

Intellectually, I know that isn't true. I mean, hell, look at Nikki and Damien—she's pursuing her dream even more now because Damien has encouraged her—but one example from one friend can't overshadow my fears.

I say none of that, but as the elevator arrives and we step on, Ryan looks at me with such tenderness that I can't help but feel he understands.

"No matter how much we love them, we all grow up surrounded by our parents' shit. You'll either be buried in it and suffocate, or use it for fertilizer and thrive."

I stare at him for a moment, then laugh. "You're right," I say. "That's probably the most profound—and disgusting—thing that I've heard in a long time." I laugh again, then lean against him when he pulls me close. "Thank you," I whisper, then sigh when he dips his head and presses a soft kiss to my hair.

The elevator lets us off on the forty-seventh floor, just three floors shy of the top level. As far as I can tell, there are only three doors on this floor, and I frown a bit as he stops in front of one with a gold plaque on the door that reads, *ES-2*.

He pulls a keycard from his wallet, then opens the door and stands aside as I enter what can only be described as paradise.

The room has a huge living area, complete with a wet bar and a grand piano. But the furnishings are nothing compared to the view—an entire wall of windows that look out on all of Las Vegas, and if I turn my head to take it all in, I can see from the Stratosphere to the Luxor and beyond.

The sun has begun to dip low in the horizon, and the light has an orange quality now, as if it is painting the town. The view is stunning, vibrant, and I turn to Ryan in wonder.

"This isn't the room that the station booked for me, is it?"

"No."

"This is a Stark International hotel."

It's not a question, but he answers anyway. "Yes."

I think back since our arrival. The way the woman welcomed him. The casino chip he had in his pocket. The fact that we didn't have to check in to get a key. Honestly, I should have realized.

"Do you live here?"

He laughs. "No, I live in LA, not far from Damien, only in a much smaller house. But I spend about four weeks out of every year here going over procedure with the staff and auditing all of our security systems and operations. This is one of the executive suites. We all have use of it."

"You always carry casino chips in your pocket?"

"No, but I do tend to keep some in the car. Once we arrived, I grabbed a few."

"Oh." That made sense. "And you have a closet or something here, which is why I'm the only one who had to buy clothes."

"Or something," he confirms. "I keep a suitcase on site. By now, housekeeping should have unpacked and pressed my clothes."

I lift a brow. "Must be nice."

"I promise you, it is."

"So how did you land such a cush job?" I ask as I stroll around the room. "I mean, heading up an entire division for Damien's umbrella company—I know the guy, and that's a pretty plum job."

"It is," Ryan says. "But I'm exceptionally good at what I do."

I pull out a bottle of wine from the fridge behind the wet bar. There is a corkscrew already sitting out, and I study Ryan as I open the wine. "I believe you. How did you get that way?"

He takes a seat, his eyes never leaving me. "Law enforcement runs in my family. My great-grandfather was in Scotland Yard, and my grandfather was MI6."

"Wow. And your dad?"

"He disappointed them by moving to Boston. Became a cop. Married a secretary at the district attorney's office."

I laugh as I cross to him, a glass of wine in each hand. "It really is all in the family."

"Which is why I was such a disappointment." He takes the wine, and I plunk myself down on the table in front of him. He sips, then smiles. "I could get used to this."

"What?"

"You, waiting on me."

I raise a brow. "I'm yours to command—at least for a few more days." I lick my lips provocatively, then very deliberately drop my gaze to his crotch. And then, because I'm feeling bold, I lean forward and cup his erection. He is already hard, and knowing that gives me a feminine thrill. "Any time you want," I whisper. "You just tell me how you want me to service you."

I see the tension on his face as he fights for control. "This will do nicely for now," he says. He nods to the floor. "Come a little closer."

I do, getting on my knees in front of him, and I keep up the rhythm, stroking his cock as he tells me his story.

"I didn't want to be a cop," he says. "Christ, Jamie, do you know what you're doing to me?"

"I have some idea," I admit. "Go on."

"But when my dad was killed in the line, that's what everyone expected of me."

I pause my hand. "I'm sorry."

"Thank you—I was young." He lays his hand on mine. "Don't stop."

I tilt my head back and meet his eyes, and for a moment I think I will get lost in them. Then he goes on, telling me about how his family rebounded—him, his sister, his mother. "But I still wasn't interested in wearing the uniform, having the badge. I considered the military, but that wasn't my thing. I trained—a lot. Martial arts, boxing, weapons. But I wasn't the military type. I wasn't the intelligence type, either. Too much chain of command, and I like being my own boss."

"What did you do?" I continue to touch him, but lightly. I want to arouse him, not overwhelm him. I want to hear his story.

"I opened a private security firm. Very high-end. Very exclusive. Very international. My family connections helped there. The company did well, and I decided to take it public. Nothing like that had ever been done before, and I caught Damien's eye. He got in contact, and to make a long story short, ended up buying me out. Since then, we've become friends, and I moved up in his company."

I frown. "So the company you started is just gone?"

"No. It's a Stark subsidiary now. I ran it for five years before taking this job. I was getting tired of globetrotting and wanted a more permanent home base. I'm thirty. I wanted to think about a life. A family."

I lick my lips and try to swallow the ball of jealousy that has caught in my throat. "A family," I repeat as I draw my hand away from his cock and lean back. "You wanted to stay in LA because of a woman?"

"No," he says, then tenderly strokes my cheek. "Not then."

I try not to react, not to read too much into those casual words. But I can't help but wonder.

His smile turns mischievous. "Actually, there is a woman, and she very much influenced my move."

I narrow my eyes. "Oh?"

"My sister is at UCLA. I like being able to see her, help her out. Spoil her rotten."

I think about my dress. About everything. "I imagine you do that very well."

"Drives her crazy," he admits cheerfully.

"What's her name?"

"Moira," he says. "Dad died when she was eight, so I've always felt a bit like a parent. She's amazing," he adds as I watch his face, studying this new side of the man who already has me falling.

He puts his hand over mine. "As much as I'm enjoying your touch," he says, "I think it's time to move on."

"Oh?" His cock is hard beneath his jeans, and I'm hoping that he has plans to put that lovely erection to very good use.

"We have dinner reservations. You should change."

"Right," I say, standing up and hoping my disappointment doesn't show.

I start to step away, but his voice stops me. "Wait," he says. "First things first."

I turn back, and there's something in his tone that makes me wary.

"You left," he said. "You ran, actually."

I lick my lips. "I thought we were past that. Our new deal. Roulette. The ball on red."

"And I'm very much enjoying our arrangement so far," he says, which is a bit baffling as so far he hasn't touched me. Not really. But that, I suppose, is all part of the tease.

But what he's talking about now...I shake my head, uncertain. "What do you want?"

"It was a bad thing you did, Jamie. We both know it."

"Maybe," I say, still wary.

"Strip."

I blink. "Excuse me?"

He leans back, his arms stretched along the rear of the couch. He looks relaxed and powerful and most definitely in charge. "I said, strip."

"Why?"

His mouth curves in a lazy, seductive smile. "Why do you think?"

My mouth has gone dry, and my knees are suddenly weak. Whatever he intends, I know that I want it—and yet still I am nervous. "I think you're going to fuck me," I say, and I can't keep the note of hope out of my voice.

"No," he says firmly. "I'm going to punish you."

"Hunter—"

He smiles. "That's it. I like that. You call me Hunter when you know what's coming."

"*Ryan,*" I say more firmly, making him laugh.

"It's no use, kitten. Hush now. Hush and take off your clothes. I promise you, Jamie, you don't want to cross me."

I am tempted to do just that simply because I want to see how far he will take this. But I also want what I know he will give me. His hands, his cock, his body.

But there will be none of that until I strip. Until he punishes me.

I remember what he'd said that first night in Malibu—how he'd talked about spanking me. I remember, too, how wet the very idea had made me.

It makes me wet now.

"Are you going to spank me?"

"No talking," he says again, "or I'll be dining alone tonight. Go on," he urges. "I want to watch you strip for me."

I don't speak, but I move back to stand in front of him. Slowly, I peel off my clothes, one garment at a time, until I am standing naked in front of him. I can see the desire in his eyes and know that he is looking forward to this.

And, yes, so am I.

I smile boldly, then slide my hand down over my sex just because I want to do a little bit of punishing myself. "I'm wet," I say, then bring my own finger to my mouth.

"Jesus, Jamie," he says, and while I have him, I decide to take the extra step and see just how crazy I can make him.

I move closer, then bend over his lap, putting my bare ass in front of him. "Spank me," I say. "You know you want to."

My pubis is pressed against his lap, and I can feel his erection grow. I close my eyes, relishing the feel of his hand rubbing a smooth circle on my rear. And then his hand is gone, replaced only moments later with a quick, sharp sting.

I cry out in both surprise and pain—and as his palm strokes quickly over the spot, I relax and breathe deep as the fingers of pain spread out, transforming to electric shocks that sizzle through me, focusing most intently on my sex, now even more hot. Even more needy.

"Do you like that?" he says, and I can tell by his growing erection that he does.

"Yes—it's..." I search for the right word. "Liberating," I finally say, and it's true. The sting, the pain, sends me flying, freeing me for an even more intense passion.

"Again," he says, then lands another smack followed in quick succession by another. He is spanking and stroking, giving pain and then pleasure. Sending me spiraling up and then reeling me back in.

I have never done this before. Never felt this before.

And I like it. Dear god, I like it.

"Hunter," I whisper as my cunt throbs in a silent demand for his touch. "Can I be bad every day?"

He laughs, then rubs his hands upon my ass, my back, my shoulders. "You are perfection, Jamie. You are delight. And as for your punishment, we'll have to see just how naughty you are. Right now, I think you've been punished enough."

I sigh, fighting my way back up through the waves of pleasure, the sweet tingle of pain and promise.

"I take it you like that?" His voice pours softly over me, strong and intoxicating, like the smooth burn of whiskey.

"Yes," I admit as my body clenches with unfulfilled need. "But please, Hunter. Will you fuck me now?"

"No," he says smoothly. "Now, I'm going to feed you."

Chapter Ten

As with the rest of the hotel, Ryan is known in the restaurant. The moment we set foot through the door, a distinguished man with graying temples and perfect posture strides toward us.

The space itself is beautiful, as is every part of this hotel that I have seen. The paneling is a deep mahogany, and the tables are draped with crisp white cloths. Sturdy, comfortable-looking chairs surround the tables, upholstered in warm red leather.

The art is appealing, hyper-realistic paintings of wine bottles and glasses, each larger than life and brimming with color. The lighting is low but not too dark, and the acoustics are good enough to hear your companions but not so good that you can eavesdrop on the next table.

Best of all, it smells incredible.

"Mr. Hunter, so good to see you again. Your usual table?"

"Not tonight, Stephen. The lady and I would like some privacy. Is station twelve available?"

"It is," Stephen says, and he leads us to a round booth in the back of the restaurant from which we can see the rest of the room, and yet we still feel secluded. It is, I think, the perfect date table.

Ryan orders wine and oysters on the half shell, and Stephen nods in acknowledgement before leaving us alone.

"If this isn't your table," I begin as soon as Stephen is out of earshot, "where do you usually sit with your women?" I add a teasing quality to my voice, but the truth is that I want to know. I am not jealous—not really. But my curiosity borders on intense.

"I've never brought a woman here," he says.

"Because you're always working when you come to Starfire?"

"No," he says. "I have access to the suite anytime."

"Oh," I say, finding that tidbit of information extremely fascinating.

He leans over and brushes a kiss over my lips. "I haven't brought a woman," he says, "because there's never been a woman I wanted to bring."

I force myself not to grin like a fool. After all, Ryan's dating history shouldn't be of any interest to me. Not now. Not with me just days away from returning to Texas.

All true, and yet I can't deny the fingers of delight that dance along my spine, making my body tingle with the knowledge that, at least as to this one small thing, I am unique and special to him.

I clear my throat so as not to show my pleasure. "I didn't realize you'd been celibate before me," I tease.

"Are you fishing, Ms. Archer?" he asks. "Should I be flattered?"

I frown. "Flattered?"

He slides his hand along my leg, making the silk of the dress rub provocatively over my skin. "That you're jealous of the other women I've dated."

I lick my lips, my legs now warm, my sex now tingling. "We're not dating."

"You're right. I'll rephrase. Are you jealous of the other women I've fucked?"

What the hell, I think, and then answer. "Yes," I say boldly. "I am."

His smile is triumphant. "Good." He tightens his fingers on my thigh then leans over and kisses my cheek. "I'll tell you a secret, kitten. I've been with a lot of women. You're the only one who has truly gotten under my skin."

I feel a rush of cold at his words, like a victim going into shock. I don't think this is fear, though. I think it is hope. Sweet, delicious, terrifying hope. "Be careful," I say quickly before he has the chance to study my silence. "You're going to break the rules. You're going to knock me off-kilter."

"I wouldn't dream of it," he says. "But I wonder if I should be the one who's jealous?"

"Maybe you should," I say flippantly. "I've fucked a lot of men."

The words come easily. Hell, *he's* easy. Maybe it's because I know that this is a temporary thing that will end when we reach Dallas. Maybe it's because he's Ryan.

Maybe it's because we started as friends even if, in some secret deep part of myself, I want to end up so much more. All I know is that this is comfortable.

He is studying my face, his expression inquisitive. "How many of them meant something to you? These men you fucked?"

"Three," I say easily. "The first because he was a genuine

friend, and we never should have been so stupid. The second I thought was real, but I was mistaken. I thought he broke my heart, but all he really did was wound my pride."

"Your friend Ollie," he says. "And the second is the asshole movie star?"

"Yup. Bryan Raine. Creep extraordinaire."

"And the third?"

I look at him, but I don't answer. Instead I just smile and sip my wine.

I think he understands, but his expression is almost sad when he says, "You burn through men like you're on a quest, kitten. What is it you expect to find?"

I shake my head. "I don't know," I say. What I want to say is *you*.

A waitress arrives with a bottle of wine, and after Ryan samples it, she pours us each a glass. I desperately want a sip, but before I can take one, Ryan twines his fingers with mine. "Maybe you don't need Texas or your plan. Maybe you just need to find a man who grounds you."

"Maybe." I shrug. "I don't know. I make bad choices."

"In the past, yes," he says. "But how long are you going to keep using that excuse as a Band-Aid on your fear?"

My head snaps up. "I'm not afraid."

"The hell you're not. You're afraid of me. You're afraid of staying."

I look away because he is right. "That's different."

He doesn't answer, probably because he knows that he's right, and my excuse is just bullshit.

I tug my hand free and then sip my wine.

"My looks are the thing that scare me the most," I say. It's not the kind of thing I usually share, but I want so much to be close to this man. Foolish, since I'm about to leave him, but I can't argue with what I want.

His smile is sweet and genuine. "There's nothing scary about your looks, kitten."

I return the smile because I know he's just putting me at ease. "I know you think I'm pretty," I say.

"Beautiful," he corrects.

"All right. I don't mind that either because I really do believe you see me. But most people..." I trail off with a shrug. "I used to be afraid that no one saw me at all. They just saw the trappings." I take another sip of wine. "I got hurt by a lot of guys once I realized they didn't give a crap about what was in my head. They only wanted my face and my tits and my body on their arm."

He reaches for my hand, then squeezes.

I shrug. "It's okay. I figured it out fast enough. And then I turned it around. Turned it into a tool. They never saw the real me anyway, so I finally decided that if I had it, I might as well use it." My smile is thin. "I believe in being pragmatic."

"Maybe so, but there is no escaping reality. And the reality is that you are beautiful. It's not a curse. It's not a tool. I've seen some of the pictures Nikki has taken of you. And captured on camera, you are truly exceptional. But it's not because you have those incredible cheekbones or the kind of mouth a guy wants to see wrapped around his cock," Ryan says, making me smirk. "You have a light, Jamie. You shine. You walk into a room and—"

"How do you do that?" I ask.

"What?"

"Make me feel special."

His smile is so gentle it makes my heart swell. "Maybe you are special."

He lifts his hand, and Stephen comes over, this time carrying a flat, square box wrapped in silver paper. "I bought you something," Ryan says to me. He takes the box from Stephen and sets it in front of me. "Open it."

"Ryan." I can't seem to stop grinning, and I reach for the box and pull it close. It is a jewelry store box, so the top is wrapped separately from the bottom. All I have to do is untie the bow and lift the lid. Inside, nestled in tissue paper, is the stunning silver collar. And on the center loop, there now hangs a lovely silver lock.

Ryan brushes his fingertip against the lock. "Because I want to lock you up and keep you. Because I will always keep you locked tight within my heart. Take your pick, Jamie. Both are equally true."

His words make tears prick at my eyes, so I focus only on the gift. "It's incredible. Thank you."

"Will you put it on?"

I remember what we said in the store. That wearing it would mean that I belong to him. "Yes," I say. "I will."

He helps me fasten it. It feels odd at first—I own a few chokers, but I don't wear them often, but I know that I will get used to it. More than that, I kind of like the fact that I feel it there against my skin. It is a reminder of what I am. Of whose I am.

"Do you like it?"

I don't have a mirror—I left my purse in the room—but I reach up and feel it, and I can imagine how it looks. That isn't what is important anyway, and when I turn to him, I am smiling. "Of course I do," I say. "It makes me yours."

I see the heat banked in his eyes as he brushes his hand over my cheek. "Yes," he says. "It does."

I lean over to kiss him, but am interrupted by the arrival of the waitress with our oysters. Ryan looks at me, and the gleam in his eye can only be described as devilish. "I didn't think to ask," he says. "Do you like oysters?"

"I've never actually had any," I admit. "Not on the half shell, anyway."

"Really?"

"Sad, isn't it?" I say with a woe-is-me tone to my voice. "I've lived such a sheltered and unadventurous life."

"Very pure," he says. "Very sheltered."

I grin.

"At any rate, it's time to add some adventure, and I do think you'll like them. Do you trust me?"

"You know I do." And now my tone is all serious.

He meets my eyes, and what I see in that brilliant blue warms me. "I'm very glad to hear it," he says.

The dozen oysters are arranged artfully on a plate surrounding a half shell full of red sauce. "Open your mouth," he says as he dips a small spoon into the sauce, then dabs it onto an oyster. "There are stories that Casanova ate fifty of these for breakfast every day," he adds, his voice low and steady.

I do as he says, opening my mouth, though I truly don't know what to expect. I trust him though. More than that, I want this moment.

His eyes never leave mine as he raises the shell to my parted lips. "That's it. Now suck, and just let it slide down your throat. Oh, Jesus, Jamie, you're killing me," he adds when I do as he demands, then use the tip of my tongue to catch the last bit of sauce.

"Delicious," I whisper, but even I'm not sure if I mean the oyster or the moment.

"You do know what they say about oysters?" Ryan asks as he lifts another one to his own mouth. "Why a man like Casanova would want so many of them?"

"Why don't you tell me," I say, though I knew perfectly well.

"They say oysters are an aphrodisiac," he says as he takes one of his own.

"Do they?" I pluck another shell up, then dab sauce on it. I draw it to my mouth, then slowly suck it in as he watches, the desire on his face so sharp it's a wonder it doesn't cut me to pieces.

I swallow, then smile sweetly as I indicate the oysters. "I'm not sure if I should be flattered you want to seduce me or insulted that you need so much help in order to try."

"Trust me," Ryan says. "There's nothing an aphrodisiac could do for me at this point that having you next to me isn't doing better."

I hear the hint of something wicked in his voice, and it sends a shiver up my spine. "I'm very glad to hear it," I say.

He takes a sip of wine. "I want you to do something for me now."

I narrow my eyes, wary. "What?"

"Take off your panties."

I lift my brows. "Um, no."

He tilts his head, his expression stern. "I seem to recall coming to an agreement as to the rules."

"My answer," I say, "is still no. Not because I'm feeling rebellious, but because I'm not wearing any."

I see the flare in his eyes that tells me I've surprised him. "Oh, really. Well, in that case..."

The hand that has been on my thigh moves up, and his fingers slip into that secret pocket. I gasp, though, when I feel the warm touch of his fingertips against my bare thigh.

I turn, shocked. "What—how—?"

"I really didn't see the point of a pocket when it was so much more convenient without that seam." He grins wickedly. "Full access."

"But—"

With his other hand, he silences me with a finger to my lips. "Spread your legs," he says.

"We're in a restaurant."

"Then I hope that when I make you come, you can refrain from screaming."

"Ryan," I say, but though my tone is a protest, my actions are not. I spread my legs, and when his hand slips down and finds me already wet, already excited, Ryan lets out a low whistle.

"You like this as much as I do," he says, "getting off in public. Knowing that you're mine. That I can touch you anywhere, make you come for me anywhere."

His fingers slide over me, and I am wet—so wet that there is no denying the truth of his words.

A waitress comes to check on our wine and asks if we'd like to order the meal. I manage a polite smile, and all the while Ryan's fingers are stroking me, dipping into me, taking me higher and higher.

As if to torment me, he asks her to recite the specials, and as she does, I reach under the table and clutch my own knee, trying to stifle the urge to squirm, to get his hand to move faster, tighter. To take me that much further.

As soon as she's gone, I round on him. "Bastard!" I snap, but he only catches my mouth in a kiss and then whispers, "Come for me. Come for me now, kitten," as he thrusts deep inside me.

I grab the edge of the table and stare blankly into space, willing my body not to move as the orgasm ripples through me. It is as if all that energy, all that explosion, remains centered in my cunt, and my body clenches and clenches around the fingers he has thrust inside me, all secret, all hidden inside my skirt and beneath the tablecloth of this fancy, five-star restaurant.

"I hate you," I say when I come down from the high.

"No," he says. "You don't." He pauses for a moment, then slides his hand out of my dress. "I have another present for you," he says.

I decide it is safer not to ask, and he reaches into his pocket and pulls out a coil of ribbon with a hook on the end.

"What is that?"

"A leash," he says with a twinkle in his eye. "It will latch onto that loop even with the lock charm on the necklace."

I smile, feeling bold. "All right," I say. "Attach it. Then lead me back to the room and fuck me properly. But Ryan, you work here. I wonder what people will think."

"Probably that I'm the luckiest man in Vegas. But you do raise a good point." He reaches over and hooks the clip to the necklace. Then he lets the ribbon trail down, tucking the long end down my cleavage so that the remainder is hidden beneath my skirt.

I raise a brow. "People will still know."

"Let them."

I lick my lips, still aroused and more than willing to take this further. "Ryan," I say. "How would you feel about skipping dinner?"

He laughs. "Sweetheart, I wouldn't mind at all."

He waits until we are out of the elevator and walking down the hall to the penthouse to pull out the leash. When he does, though, I like it. There's pleasure in belonging to him, comfort in knowing that he is there. That I can rely on him. Go to him.

Talk to him.

A twinge of regret pokes at me as I remember that this is only temporary. But I push it soundly away. Right now, I am living only in the moment. Only in our arrangement.

I pause in the doorway despite the tug on the leash. He turns to look at me, mock disapproval on his face, and I smile. "Please, sir," I say, and watch his mouth quirk with amusement. "Will you take me to the window?"

He does, and we stand together, looking out onto the brightly lit Las Vegas skyline.

"All the women in the world," I begin. "You could have any of them, you know."

"Not any," he says. "Probably just ninety percent. Ninety-five tops."

I smile, then sober. "You chose me."

He moves behind me, then presses his hands to my shoulders

and kisses the top of my head. "No kitten," he says. "We chose each other."

I turn and look out the window again. "Yeah," I say to our reflection. "We did."

I tilt my head and smile at him, then trail my fingers from the choker, down the leash, to his hand. "So now that you've led me here, what do you intend to do with me?"

"Oh, I think we can think of something," he says, and then unfastens my halter and unzips the back of the dress. It falls off me like so much gossamer, leaving me naked except for the silver collar, the lock, the red ribbon leash, and my three-inch heeled sandals.

"That," he says, "is a very pretty picture."

He gives the leash a tug, pulling me to him. I stumble into his arms, laughing, then kick off the heels.

"Maybe I'll just have you serve me wine and cheese like that."

"I would. But I think you can do better."

"Oh, I think I can, too," he says, then unclips the leash. He takes the ribbon and coils it in his hands. "Turn around, Jamie," he says, and I comply willingly.

"Now close your eyes."

I do, and then feel the gentle brush of the ribbon as he wraps it around my eyes—once, twice, three times, until it is at least as effective as a traditional blindfold. Then he pulls me down, laying me out on a soft, fur rug.

I wait for his touch, but it doesn't come. At least not at first. Then I hear the subtle shift in the air and hear the clink of ice in a glass.

"Do you like bourbon, kitten?" he asks, and when I nod, I

find his finger on my lip. I draw it in, suckling, and listen as the pattern of his breathing changes with his growing excitement.

Gently, he pulls his finger away, then trails it down my belly. When he gets to my navel, I arch up, surprised by the quick, cold shock of an ice cube.

"You're delicious," he says, and I tremble in awareness as he licks and kisses his way down the trail, then sucks at my bellybutton, the sensation making me a little crazy.

"I want to make love to you," he says, and there is so much gentleness in his voice it seems to get into my heart and squeeze.

I reach for him, but he simply says, "no," and I put my arms back. "Not yet. Not until I'm sure you're ready."

"I'm ready," I say. "I'm always ready for you."

His answer is a murmur, and then he is upon me. Gently, sweetly. Hands, mouth. He strokes me, plays me, touches and teases me. If his goal is to turn me into nothing more than pure awareness, pure need, then he has accomplished it fully.

I am melting, wanting. And what I want is more.

"Please," I beg. "If I can't see you, at least let me touch you."

Gently, he lifts my hand and presses it to his chest. It is bare, and I stroke lightly over the smattering of chest hair. I find his back with my other hand and stroke down, delighting at the firmness of his tight, bare ass beneath my fingers.

"I can't wait," he says. "I want you, kitten, and I'm taking you now."

"Yes," I whisper, lifting my hips and spreading my legs. I want him in me, on top of me. I want to lose myself under the weight of him, to feel consumed by him.

He strokes me first, his fingers readying me, and I moan in

pleasure and anticipation. Then I feel the head of his cock at my sex, the pressure of entry, and then the sweet thrill when he drives himself home.

We move together, anticipating touches, sharing kisses. It is sensual, romantic, soft and easy. He is right—we are making love, and that sweet reality makes me want to weep with joy even as much as it scares me.

He strokes me, bringing me higher and higher until I tremble in his arms, the orgasm rippling over me this time like waves upon a sunlit pond.

His coming is much more violent, and he cries my name as he finds his release, and I cling to him, urging him deeper and deeper, wanting every last bit of him.

We lay together, and he takes off my blindfold then smiles down at me. Then he pulls me close and holds me.

I sigh with delight and contentment. And as I curl up against him, I try not to think of how much I want to stay with him, and that all of this is leading to the one inevitable conclusion—me in Texas, and Ryan in California.

Chapter Eleven

I'm floating on an undulating sea, rising and falling, each wave battering my body and taking me closer, closer, closer to shore.

The water is warm and wet, slick and sensual. It moves over my naked skin. Teasing, seducing. Claiming.

It will suck me under, I know that, and yet I don't care. I want to drown it it, I want to go down, down, down...

"Hunter," I whisper as I slide out of sleep. My eyes flutter open, and I look up into the dark heat of his eyes.

His hands are pressed into the mattress on either side of my head, supporting his body as he moves slowly, languidly inside me. My body is alive—awake. Certainly more awake than the rest of me, though I'm getting there fast.

I spread my legs wider, giving him access, silently acknowledging that he has taken me in sleep—and that I like it.

He thrusts harder, again and again, until finally he explodes above me, and I watch as the orgasm draws him up, and then crashes him down upon me.

When his breathing returns to normal, he gently brushes his

lips over mine. "Good morning."

I smile in return. "Nice way to wake up."

"You're at my mercy, after all," he says. "And I couldn't resist you naked and sprawled on your back, your legs parted, just beckoning for me. You were already wet," he said. "Wet and slick and hot before I even touched you."

"I was dreaming of you," I admit. "And then I was dreaming of this." I lick my lips, then swallow, foolishly embarrassed by what I am about to say. "I like it. I want to be used."

I see the heat flare in his eyes. "Do you. Why?"

I start to turn my head away, but he stops me with a firm finger on my chin.

"Why," he repeats.

"You know," I say. "It's because I'm yours." And then, because I have not yet had enough of him, I turn over, tucking my knees under me so that I am giving him my rear.

"I'm yours," I say, my voice low and meaningful. I look back over my shoulder. "Please. I want you. I want you first."

"Jamie, kitten." His voice is raw, and there's no mistaking the desire. "I don't want to hurt you. If you've never...without lube..."

"My purse," I say. "A holdover from my days of fucking around," I add, then smile when he smirks.

It takes him only a moment to find it, and then he is back. "You're sure?"

I want to tell him that I don't want to leave him. That I think, just maybe, I have fallen in love with him.

But that isn't something I can say, and it's not something I can give. But I can give him me. "Yes," I say. "Please, yes."

"Then come here," he says, pulling me up from my position

on my knees. He crushes his mouth against mine in a kiss that is wild and deep and crazed with passion.

"I adore you," he says when we come up for air. "I want you. Hell, I want you more than I've ever wanted any woman. Christ, I'm hard again."

"You have me," I say as he moves down my body, stroking and suckling my breasts, then laving my sex with quick, fluttery kisses until I am squirming, so close to bursting I can feel the hum of the approaching climax in my blood.

"Turn over," he says. "Like you were, on your knees."

I comply, and his hands stroke my back, soft and sensual as if I am some fragile thing. His finger trails down further, and he explores my rear, his lubed finger sliding over me, easing inside me, readying me.

I close my eyes, my body trembling. I am not a stranger to anal play, but I have never had a man inside me. I'm glad. I want to have Ryan, and only Ryan, and now, as he gets me slick and ready, I try to relax. I concentrate on the throbbing anticipation in my cunt. In the tightness of my nipples. On the delicious sensitivity of my skin.

"You're ready, baby," he says, and I close my eyes, relaxing, opening for him as he presses his cock against my tight entrance. Slowly, he eases inside, and I suck in air, wanting him to stop, and yet at the same time wanting more.

"Am I hurting you?" he asks as he moves slowly and deliberately.

"No," I lie, because the pain is part of it. Like when he spanked my ass, the pain is mixed with pleasure, and I want it all. "It's okay. Please. More. Don't stop."

He takes me at my word, still moving carefully, but thrusting more intensely until, finally, my body seems to welcome him, and the pain melts in to something red and silky, like a memory of pain turned to pleasure.

I shift my arm so that I can tease my clit, getting closer and closer along with him. I come quickly, my body too aware, too ready, and every part of me clenches, drawing him in even tighter and wresting a long, low groan from him.

He comes after me, and when he does, he cries my name, then draws me close and holds me tight. "Kitten," he murmurs, his lips pressed to my neck. "Thank you."

"For what?" I ask, and his answer fills me to bursting: "For you."

* * * *

Later, in the shower, he tenderly strokes my cheek. "You are amazing," he says.

"I'm glad you think so," I tease. "I feel amazing."

It's true. My body feels thoroughly fucked, deliciously used. And simply having Ryan beside me is pleasure enough. The fact that he's also naked adds on serious bonus points.

"Yeah," I repeat, and then kiss him. "I feel amazing."

When we get out of the shower, he is dressed and looking sinfully handsome in under fifteen minutes.

I take a bit longer to put together. Especially since today is my interview with Ellison Ward.

I spend an hour doing my makeup for the camera, then dressing, then checking myself in the mirror. I'm not naïve—I know that Ward is the one who will get the screen time—but I also know this gig is potentially a break for me, and I don't want to fuck it up.

"You look stunning," Ryan says. "Professional, sexy, feminine and smart. All excellent qualities as far as I'm concerned."

"I appreciate the endorsement," I say, then accept his kiss, though I make him kiss me on the cheek so as to not muck up my lipstick.

The collar is on the counter where I left it before showering, and now I pick it up. I want to wear it, but it really doesn't go with my camera-ready outfit. I'm about to say that to Ryan—to tell him why I'm not wearing this gift that so moved me—when he takes it from me.

"What are you—" I begin, but he hushes me with a single press of a fingertip to my lips. Then he uses a small pocket knife to remove the lock from the loop on the collar. He puts the necklace back, then presses the lock into my hand. "You hold the key to my heart," he says as I melt just a little. "Keep it safe."

I nod, then put the lock gently in the pocket of my jacket. The weight is minimal, but I can feel it there, and it bolsters my confidence.

As we are leaving the suite, a bellman arrives and hands me a valet ticket. "Your Ferrari, Ms. Archer."

"Thank you," I say, but I'm looking at Ryan.

"My guys brought it in," he says. "The gas gauge is still off, but the tank's full. I wanted to ask before I sent her ahead to Texas, but just so you know, you'll be driving there with me."

I smile. "Perfect," I say. What I don't say is that it would be perfect, except for the part where we leave each other at the end.

I drop the valet ticket into my purse for the time being, then follow Ryan to the elevator.

He goes with me to the interview, which is being held in Ward's penthouse suite. We take the elevator to the top floor, then enter a suite that looks much like our own—only significantly more crowded.

My cameraman is already there, as are at least half a dozen people who must perform some function on the film, though I have no clue what. Another five or six people hover around a buffet that has been set up on the far side of the room, in front of the windows. A few more are huddled around a table spread with papers that I think are pages of a screenplay.

I do not see Ellison Ward.

A harried woman with pencils sticking out of her messy, blond topknot comes hurrying over. She glances at her wrist, says, "I'm Birgit, and we're already running late," even though I'm five minutes early, and hustles me to a small sofa. The cameraman leaves his post to come over and shake my hand.

"Leo," he says. "I'll shoot Ellison, and then we'll go back and reshoot you asking the questions. Don't wanna miss a chance of getting something prime on the celeb, so it works out best that way."

"Fine," I say. "Where is our celeb?"

Beside me, Birgit glances at her watch. "He better be on his way or we are going to be seriously off schedule." She pulls a walkie-talkie off her belt. "Dammit, Carson, I need Ellison."

"On our way," comes the crackly reply.

A few feet behind Leo, Ryan leans against a pillar watching me. I catch his eye and smile. At that particular moment, everything feels right. The job. The man. Life in general. I wish I could bottle it and keep it tight against my chest.

But I should know it's too good to last because when the double doors to the connecting room open, Ellison Ward and his entourage emerge. And there, standing right behind my subject, is Bryan Raine.

I must have reacted because Ryan takes one look at my face, then turns to look behind him. When he turns back to me, it's clear that he understands. His face is hard, and I am quite certain that if he could kill Raine and get away with it, Ryan wouldn't even hesitate.

Honestly, that feels kind of nice.

I have no idea why Raine is there—he wasn't on the cast list of the movie I received—and I'm really not up to speculating. It's bad enough that he's hovering nearby like some huge, dark spider, just waiting to trap me and suck me dry.

But my fears are foolish. He may have entered the room, but he doesn't stay, and when I look around for him, there is no sign.

I say a silent thank you to fate and the universe, then shake hands with Ellison Ward. He's charming and polite and very properly British. He puts me at ease immediately and the interview seems to sing. He is honest and forthright, and I'm able to work in both the fluff questions and also dig deeper.

By the time it wraps, I am feeling incredible about myself, about Ellison, and about the world in general.

I say good-bye to Ellison, then sit while Leo has me run through my questions again. When he's finished, Ryan approaches, and it's all I can do not to throw myself into his arms.

"You were wonderful," he says.

"She was," Leo agrees. "Got a way with the camera, too.

You're gonna do good, Jamie. Hope we work together again."

"Thank you," I say, then invite him to join us for a drink in the hotel bar. He declines, and I'm secretly grateful. I would have been happy to have him along, but I'm happier to have Ryan all to myself.

"A drink," he says as we ride the elevator down. "I had planned to buy you a celebratory trip to Paris, but if you'd rather have this instead..."

I laugh, then pull him in close for another kiss. I'm still laughing when we get out of the elevator car, and my good mood lasts until we reach the middle of the lobby.

It fades there because Bryan Raine is coming right toward us.

"Jamie," he says. "Sorry I didn't get the chance to say hello upstairs. I've got a part in Johnson's next movie, and he wanted me to drive in and take a look at some pages. Maybe we can grab a drink? Catch up?"

I clutch Ryan's hand tight. "No," I say. "I really don't think so."

I continue walking, holding onto Ryan for support. "Asshole," I mutter as we reach the lobby bar. "Look at me," I say as we take a seat. "I was in a great mood, and he went and fucked it up."

"Hey," Ryan says, giving my hand a squeeze. "Forget about him."

I nod. "I know. You're right. Shit." I stand up again. "Order me something fabulous. I'm going to run to the ladies' room."

I take off that way, then spend the next five minutes staring at myself in the mirror and asking myself what the fuck is wrong with me.

When I come out, I'm calmer—at least until I see Bryan standing by Hunter, looking about as trapped as a gazelle being stalked by a lion. Hunter says something else, and then Bryan takes off like a shot, not even noticing me as he rushes past.

"What the hell?" I say to Hunter as soon as I arrive.

"I told him to keep the fuck away," he says, then takes a sip of his Scotch. "I got you a Cosmopolitan. It seemed like a fun treat."

I, however, am not interested in the drink. "You just sent him away?"

"Yes," Ryan says.

I shake my head, a little bit baffled, a little bit angry. Honestly, I'm not sure what I'm feeling other than a little pissed off. Hadn't I already taken care of the asshole myself?

"I don't need you to step in to play guard dog for me," I say. "I dealt with the guy myself, didn't I? I'm not one of your job responsibilities."

"You're right," he says, and his tone is clipped enough that I can tell he's irritated, too. "You're not a job responsibility. You're the woman I love."

I freeze, his words hitting me with the force of a slap. Automatically, I shake my head. *The woman I love.*

I want to believe it—god, how I want to believe it. But it can't be true. And even if it is...

I run my fingers through my hair. "Hunter," I say. "Hunter, don't."

"I love you, Jamie. Stay. Don't go to Texas. Stay with me."

I am shaking my head, fighting to make reason take over, because if I run solely on emotion, I know I will be lost. That's the old Jamie, after all. The one who fucks up. The one who gets all twisted around and makes a mess of her life and has to run home to Mom and Dad to get her head back on straight.

The new Jamie *thinks*.

But damned if the new Jamie knows what to think about this.

He looks blurry, and I realize that I am crying. Brutally, I wipe the tears away with the back of my hand. How can I be so miserable, I wonder. This man loves me. And yet...

"You can't possibly," I whisper. "You barely know me."

True. Yet wasn't I falling in love with him, too? Hadn't I told myself that already? Wasn't I already trying to hide from reality?

"We barely know each other," I add, this time speaking to the both of us.

"Why does it have to take time to fall in love?" Ryan asks. "If the push is hard enough, the fall is going to be fast."

I only look at him, wanting to believe.

"And has it really been that fast, Jamie?"

"We haven't even dated," I protest.

"I'm not the least bit interested in dating you. Dating suggests an exploration. A process of discovery. But I already know you, Jamie. I know you, and I want you. And I love you."

He takes my hand, and for a moment all is right with the world. But then I glance across the bar, across the lobby. I see Bryan Raine arguing with a bellman, and my stomach twists as I am reminded what a mess I am.

Raine is the epitome of what I am running from—bad decisions.

But how the hell do I know if Ryan Hunter is a good decision or a bad one?

"I'm sorry," I say as I tug my hand free. I want to say he is everything I have ever hoped for. I want to say that I love him.

Instead, I say, "I have to think. I'm sorry, Ryan. I have to go."

Chapter Twelve

The highway stretches out in front of me, and I keep driving, thinking that if I can just get a little farther, maybe to that next mile marker, I will figure it out. But the highway always stays ahead of me, and there is always another mile marker, and I fear that I am thinking too hard.

What am I doing?

I know the answer, of course. I'm running.

What I can't figure out is why.

I tell myself that I am right to leave him. Maybe not forever, but for a while. While I get my head together. While I stick with The Plan.

Because isn't the point of The Plan to keep me from doing exactly what has happened with Ryan—to keep me from getting twisted up with a guy?

That's true—except it's not.

Because Ryan hasn't twisted me up. If anything, he's untangled me.

I reach into my pocket and close my hand around the lock as tears sting my eyes. What am I doing? Who in their right mind runs from love?

Because I do love him. More important, I know that he truly loves me.

I lift my foot off the accelerator, cringing a bit when I realize that I've pushed the Ferrari past one hundred. But she really is a sweet ride.

I slow, planning to turn the car around and head back, but something isn't right.

Once again, the car is making an odd noise, although this time when I listen more closely, I realize that the *thwump-thwump* isn't coming from the Ferrari, but from somewhere outside the car.

Frowning, I glance at the land off the shoulder. It is mostly dirt, but that dirt is billowing now, blowing and blustering, forming small dirt devils that spin and spin.

A shadow passes over. And I slam on the brakes as a sleek black helicopter with *Stark International* emblazoned on the side lands on the shoulder ahead of me.

I kill the engine and race out of the car. I don't see him, not yet, but I don't slow. I know he is there. I know he came for me.

And then there he is, jumping from the helicopter to the asphalt below. He ducks to avoid the wind that the still-spinning blades are kicking up, and when he is clear, he makes a twirling motion and the helicopter ascends once again.

I throw myself in his arms. "You came for me," I say, my voice soft with wonder.

"I will always come for you." He kisses me. A hard, deep kiss that claims me as his own, and that I feel profoundly all the way down to my toes.

Even after we break the kiss, I cling to him, wanting to reassure myself that he is real. "I was about to turn around and come back." I tilt my head up at him. "I needed to get to you. To tell you. I love you, too, Ryan Hunter."

His smile lights his eyes. "I know."

"And I found the answer," I add.

"Who is Jamie?"

I nod. "She's yours," I say, and though I expect his answering smile, his words come as a surprise.

"No," he says. "She is her own. But I am the man who loves her."

His words move me, and I pull him close and kiss him again.

"Do you still want me to take you to Texas?" he asks when we reach the car.

I shake my head. "I'm going to call Georgia. I'm not going to take the job."

He has opened the passenger door for me, but now he pauses and takes my chin in his hand. "You're sure?"

"It's a great opportunity," I say. "But only if I want to be in Texas. But I don't want to be there. I want to be in Los Angeles. I want to be with you."

I meet his eyes as I say it, and he looks back at me with so much love and tenderness I think my heart will burst.

"Ever since she made the offer," I continue, "I've been looking at it as a way to get back into the LA market. Looking past the job itself and to the future. But you're my future, Ryan. You're what I want. And so long as I'm with you, I can wait for the right job to come along. I can—"

"Shhh," he says, and then crushes his mouth to mine once again.

"Mmm," I say. "I can get used to that."

"Then we'll have to be sure to mix things up, won't we? Wouldn't want life to become predictable."

"No, we wouldn't. You know," I add, still thinking about the job. "Maybe I'll suggest that I be their LA correspondent. I'm pretty kick ass, you know. They'd be lucky to have me."

"They would," he says. "I know I am."

Across the highway there is a billboard advertising a Vegas wedding chapel. Ryan nods toward it, then gazes down at me. "I'm going to marry you someday," he says softly. The words and his voice send shivers of anticipation through me. And not even the slightest bit of fear.

"Yes," I say, "you are." And despite the fact that ours has been such a whirlwind romance it makes my head spin, I know that it is true. "But not like that," I say, nodding to the sign.

"No," he agrees. "Our wedding will be an event. A party."

"A celebration," I say, and then kiss him again simply because I have to. "I hope Damien pays you well," I add with a laugh. "Because I just spent the last few weeks doing all sorts of wedding planning with Nikki, and that means I have lots of ideas."

His mouth quirks into a smile. "Whatever you want, Ms. Archer."

"All I want is you."

"That works out well, then, because you have me. For now, for always."

I sigh and slide into his arms, feeling loved and safe and centered.

Behind us, the highway stretches on, but I don't need it. I know exactly where I'm going.

"I'm going to make you very happy," I say.

"Kitten," he says. "You already do."

Sign up for the 1001 Dark Nights Newsletter
and be entered to win a Tiffany Lock necklace.
There's a contest every quarter!

Visit www.1001DarkNights.com/key/ to subscribe.

As a bonus, all newsletter subscribers will receive a free
1001 Dark Nights story:

The First Night
by Shayla Black, Lexi Blake & M.J. Rose

Turn the page for a full list of the
1001 Dark Nights fabulous novellas...

1001 Dark Nights

FOREVER WICKED
A Wicked Lovers Novella
by Shayla Black

CRIMSON TWILIGHT
A Krewe of Hunters Novella
by Heather Graham

CAPTURED IN SURRENDER
A MacKenzie Family Novella
by Liliana Hart

SILENT BITE: A SCANGUARDS WEDDING
A Scanguards Vampire Novella
by Tina Folsom

DUNGEON GAMES
A Masters and Mercenaries Novella
by Lexi Blake

AZAGOTH
A Demonica Novella
by Larissa Ione

NEED YOU NOW
by Lisa Renee Jones

SHOW ME, BABY
A Masters of the Shadowlands Novella
by Cherise Sinclair

ROPED IN
A Blacktop Cowboys ® Novella
by Lorelei James

TEMPTED BY MIDNIGHT
A Midnight Breed Novella
by Lara Adrian

THE FLAME
by Christopher Rice

CARESS OF DARKNESS
A Phoenix Brotherhood Novella
by Julie Kenner

Also from Evil Eye Concepts
TAME ME
A Stark International Novella
by J. Kenner

Acknowledgments from the Author

I am grateful every day to all of the wonderful, incredible, amazing fans of the Stark Trilogy. Thanks so much for joining me on the journey. And a special thanks to Liz and MJ for helping me to bring Jamie's story to all of you!

About J. Kenner

Julie Kenner (aka J. Kenner and J.K. Beck) is the *New York Times*, *USA Today*, *Publishers Weekly*, and *Wall Street Journal* bestselling author of over forty novels, novellas and short stories in a variety of genres.

Praised by *Publishers Weekly* as an author with a "flair for dialogue and eccentric characterizations," JK writes a range of stories including super sexy romances, paranormal romance, chick lit suspense and paranormal mommy lit. Her foray into the latter, *Carpe Demon: Adventures of a Demon-Hunting Soccer Mom* by Julie Kenner, is in development as a feature film with 1492 Pictures.

Her recent trilogy of erotic romances, The Stark Trilogy (as J. Kenner), reached as high as #2 on the *New York Times* list, is published in over twenty countries, and is an international bestseller.

JK lives in Central Texas, with her husband, two daughters, and several cats. She loves hearing from readers, hangs out far too much on social media, and is easily bribed with coffee.

HEATED

by J. Kenner
Most Wanted, Book 2
Coming June 3, 2014!

"Shall I tell you?" he asked. "Shall I tell you exactly what I want? Exactly what I will have from you?"

His mouth was beside my ear, so close I could feel the brush of his lips as his words teased me. I didn't want to be entranced—didn't want to feel my body go soft with longing. But dammit, he was drawing me under, and soon I was going to drown in the swell of his words.

"Shall I go over in intimate detail how I will touch you? The way my fingertips will tease your nipples. How my tongue will dance over the curve of your ear. Will it make you wet to know how hard I am? How much I want to sink deep inside of you."

I made a little sound. I think I meant it to be a yes.

His hands eased lower, sliding down to my waist, then behind to cup my rear. He drew me in, nestling my sex against his thigh, and pressing so tight against me I could feel the hard bulge of his erection against my lower belly. I reached out to steady myself, and found the edges of two serving tables. I clutched at them, desperate to hold on, because I knew damn well that if I let go, I'd melt into a puddle on the floor.

"I imagine you taste like honey," Tyler murmured. "And when I slide my tongue between your legs, I'll lose myself in the sweetness of you. I want to watch your face as the orgasm builds inside you. I want to feel you tremble beneath me. And when you finally explode, I want to hold you in my arms and let my kisses pull you back together."

I trembled, my body hot and sizzling. I was aroused, my breasts heavy, my sex aching. I wanted his touch—wanted him to do all the things he was saying.

Hell, I simply wanted.

I breathed in. Once, twice. I needed to gather myself, my thoughts. I needed to maintain at least some illusion that he hadn't completely destroyed me with nothing more than words.

"Wow," I finally managed. "You don't waste time, do you?"

His smile was slow and lazy. "As far as I'm concerned, time is the one thing too precious to waste."

He stroked my cheek, my hair. His fingers twined in my curls as he played and stroked. Tighter and tighter, not enough to hurt, but enough so that I gasped in surprise when he tugged my head back and met my eyes. There was ice in the blue now. A cold, winter storm, the chill of which laced his voice as well. "Tell me the truth, Sloane. Are you wasting my time?"

I felt the blood pump through me, the rush filling my head. Not fear—not really. This was excitement. Challenge. And, yes, a bit of frustration, too, because the victory I'd so greedily claimed had apparently been premature.

"Let go of me," I said, my voice matching the ice of his eyes. "I don't know what you're talking about."

He released his grip on my hair and took a step back. I used the motion of standing up straight to shake off my nerves. Despite my desperately pounding heart, right then, this was all about playing it cool. Just like in a suspect interrogation, I wasn't about to let him see that he'd shaken me.

"I know what my game is," he said. "I'm trying to figure out yours."

"I'm not playing a game."

"Everyone's playing a game." There was no humor in his voice.

I said nothing. I'd already denied. Repeating myself would get me nowhere.

"A lot of people want a piece of me, Sloane. What do you want? An introduction? A loan? I want to know why you're here. I want to know what you want."

Slowly, I shook my head. "I'm not gold-digging, if that's what you think. And I already told you what I want. Hell, you've already told me what I want." I took a single step forward, then pressed my hand over his cock, hard inside his tailored slacks.

I watched his face as I touched him, not moving, simply touching. "'I want to feel you tremble beneath me.' That's what you said. That's what I want, too. Christ, Tyler, isn't it obvious what I want? Why I came here? I want you."

Beneath my hand, I felt his cock stiffen. He glanced down, then back at me. His face was all hard lines and angles, as if he was fighting for control. "Don't move," he said. "Don't even breathe."

"I—"

"No." His finger pressed against my lip before skimming downward. Over my chin, down my neck until he delicately traced my collar bone. Then lower, teasing my nipple with slow circles as I sucked in air and bit my lip in defense against the sounds of pleasure that wanted so desperately to escape.

The bodice was a halter, with two triangles of material attached to the waist, then rising up to tie behind my neck. He followed the material up, his finger skimming under the bow at the base of my neck.

"Shall I untie it? Let it fall? Shall I close my mouth over your bare breast right now, tease your nipple between my teeth? Tell me the truth, Sloane, would that make you hot?"

I swallowed. My mouth was so dry. I thought of the waitstaff. Of camera phones. Of the internet and the image of us, his mouth on my breast, my head back, my lips parted in pleasure. I thought of it, and I felt the quickening in my belly. The clenching in my sex.

I thought—and I whispered the only answer I could. "Yes."

"Good girl," he said, as his hand sneaked down, leaving my dress intact. I breathed a sigh of relief, then gasped as he traced his way down my cleavage, his hand slipping beneath the material just long enough for his fingers to tease and for the heat of his palm to cup my breast.

"Tyler," I moaned when he withdrew his hand, leaving me clutching the tables on either side of me, because if I let go, I would surely fall.

"Hush," he said, as he moved closer. His hand snaked around my waist to find the zipper at the back of the dress, then slowly eased it down. "Now spread your legs," he ordered as he slid his palm inside my dress, over my lower back, and then down to the curve of my ass.

I wore a stretchy lace thong, and he stroked my bare skin before finding the thin, damp strip of material ·between my legs and tugging it aside. I heard the desperate sound of my own whimper as he teased me, then sucked in a gasp as he slid a finger easily inside me and my body clenched tight around him.

He groaned in satisfaction. "Christ, you're wet," he said, his voice raw. "I don't doubt you want me, Sloane. And god knows I want you, too." He stroked my sex once, twice, then withdrew his hand, and I had to bite my lower lip in order to silence my protest. "But there's something else going on in that pretty head of yours," he added, as he zipped up my skirt, leaving me wanting and confused and frustrated. "And I will find out your secret."

He stepped back from me, then paused to look me up and down. I could only imagine what he saw. Clothes askew. Skin flushed. But I lifted my head, determined to hold my own.

He moved to the door, and pulled it part of the way open. The sounds of the party wafted in, echoing in the service hall. His eyes locked on mine, and for a moment I saw the true depth and power of this man who held so much of Chicago in his hand.

"I'll give you what you want, Sloane," he said. "What we both want. But think long and hard before you come to me. There are things that I like. Things that I want and expect from the woman in my bed. And I don't play by anyone's rules but my own."

Also from J. Kenner

Stark Trilogy

Release Me
Claim Me
Complete Me

Take Me (A Stark Trilogy novella)

Stark International
Tame Me: A Stark International Novella

Most Wanted Series

Wanted
Heated (coming soon!)
Ignited (coming soon!)

Shadow Keepers (J. Kenner writing as J.K. Beck)

When Blood Calls
When Pleasure Rules
When Wicked Craves
Shadow Keepers: Midnight (e-novella)
When Passion Lies
When Darkness Hungers
When Temptation Burns

Writing as Julie Kenner

Demon-Hunting Soccer Mom Series

Carpe Demon
California Demon
Demons Are Forever
The Demon You Know (short story)
Deja Demon
Demon Ex Machina
Pax Demonica (coming soon!)

Superhero Series

The Cat's Fancy (prequel)
Aphrodite's Kiss
Aphrodite's Passion
Aphrodite's Secret
Aphrodite's Flame
Aphrodite's Embrace

Blood-Lily Chronicles

Tainted
Torn
Turned

On behalf of 1001 Dark Nights,
Liz Berry and M.J. Rose would like to thank ~

Doug Scofield
Steve Berry
Richard Blake
Dan Slater
Asha Hossain
Chris Graham
Kim Guidroz
BookTrib After Dark
Jillian Stein
and Simon Lipskar

CPSIA information can be obtained at www.ICGtesting.com
Printed in the USA
LVOW06s1625160915

454435LV00004B/784/P